HOW TO MARRY A WEREWOLF

(IN 10 EASY STEPS)

A CLAW & COURTSHIP NOVELLA

BY GAIL CARRIGER

STORIES SET IN GAIL'S STEAMPUNK PARASOVERSE
The Delightfully Deadly Novellas
Stand-alone romance novellas featuring polite lady assassins

The Supernatural Society Novellas
LBGTQ stand-alone romance novellas with proper subversive
activities

The Claw & Courtship Novellas
Stand-alone romances featuring werewolves in cravats and the
ladies who love them

The Finishing School Series
Young adult novels, begins with *Etiquette & Espionage*
(spies, girl power, flying food)

The Parasol Protectorate Series
Five novels, begins with *Soulless*
(adventure, love, silly hats)

The Custard Protocol Series
Ongoing, begins with *Prudence*
(world travel, romance, stolen tea)

The Curious Case of the Werewolf That Wasn't
Short story set in steampunk Egypt
(featuring one sexy and rather unpleasant Italian)

GAIL'S OTHER WORKS
Fairy Debt
YA fantasy comedy short story
(girl power, dragons, and cupcakes)

My Sister's Song
High fantasy historical short story
(warrior woman takes on a Roman legion alone)

AS G. L. CARRIGER

The San Andreas Shifters Series
Blue jokes, raunchy sex, and gentle hearts
(loving werewolf meets smart-mouthed mates)

Marine Biology: San Andreas Shifter Prequel
Sweet romance gay short story
(geeky werewolf meets hot merman)
FREE with Gail's newsletter

HOW TO MARRY A WEREWOLF

(IN 10 EASY STEPS)

A CLAW & COURTSHIP NOVELLA

GAIL CARRIGER

GAIL CARRIGER LLC

GAIL CARRIGER, LLC

ACKNOWLEDGEMENTS

With grateful thanks to my pack of pigeons full of Alphas, Betas, and even a few Gammas. They averted a major breach in the Parasolverse space time continuum.

A Note on Chronology

Claw & Courtship novellas can be read in any order. This book can be enjoyed without having read any of Gail's other works.

Set in the spring of 1895 this story occurs after events chronicled in *Romancing the Werewolf* and contemporaneous with those of *Competence*. Channing is first introduced to readers in the second Parasol Protectorate book, *Changeless*. He also appears briefly in *Romancing the Inventor*.

STEP ONE

Make Yourself Readily Available

April 1896

When a young American lady of good standing is indiscreet, kind parents retire her quietly to the country with a maiden aunt and a modest stipend. Faith's parents decided to marry her off to a werewolf.

"Though you're too soiled for even those unnatural beasts." Faith's mother was not looking at her. Mrs. Wigglesworth hadn't really looked at her daughter for nearly two months. Faith was more reassured by this than not. To be noticed might tempt her mother's temper, and that was never pretty.

So, she was careful with her words. "Now, Mother, I don't think they quibble about such things, so long as I'm fresh meat."

"None of your lip, girl. That's what got you into this predicament." Faith's mother had a voice like cracked peppercorns and the face of an offended jackrabbit – all ears, red-rimmed eyes, and wrinkled nose.

No, it isn't what got me here, thought Faith. *In fact, it was the opposite. If I'd said something – if I'd lied about it – there would have been shame but no ruination.*

"Face it, my dear, she's spoiled goods by everyone's standards. Even the werewolves." Mr Wigglesworth chewed his overcooked beef wetly, with a sound like the squelching of boots in a vat of gravy.

"I don't know where we went wrong with her. The others all turned out well enough." Mrs Wigglesworth gave a long-suffering sigh. "I did so well with them, and then this one. Rotten to the core."

Faith looked down at her food. It sat untouched. She didn't feel like eating; nothing worked to fill that odd lingering emptiness. Certainly not beef, at any rate. She speared a potato and ruminated over its roundness.

They must be desperate to be rid of me, she thought, *to be considering werewolves. Or Mother hates werewolves so much, she would use me to punish them.*

Prior to this particular conversation, Faith could not remember the word *werewolf* ever spoken in the Wigglesworth household, let alone at the dinner table. For while the packs may have helped the North with their Union troubles, they still weren't considered civilized. Now they weren't even allowed into the city without escort. A werewolf was lower than a Californian, all things considered – rough rural hillbillies with too much hair. And open shirt collars. And no table manners.

Faith shivered in titillated horror. Werewolves were not permitted in any of Boston society's conservatories, let alone received into drawing rooms. Certainly not by the Wigglesworths. No one would make the mistake of calling Faith's papa a progressive. But he was a pragmatist. And everyone in Boston now knew of his daughter's shame. And Faith's mother? Well, she made no bones about her hatred for the beasts.

Her mother's hand, suddenly and without warning, slapped the table. "Don't play with your food, girl." She barked the words so sharply that spittle sprayed the table.

Faith put down her fork.

Her mother went back to *not* looking at Faith. Already, in one of those lightning mood switches that had so terrified Faith as a child, Mrs Wigglesworth was directing soft lips and coy eyes at her husband and his indifference. "You see what a bother she is to me? To this family?"

"So, how do we safely dispose of her?" Mr Wigglesworth asked his wife, because it really was Mrs Wigglesworth's responsibility. A daughter embroiled in scandal was of little political value to him. He'd never paid Faith any attention anyway, not until her indiscretion.

Mrs Wigglesworth sighed again, louder and with more force. "We must still try for an advantageous match. Your cousin offers us a relatively inexpensive option – a London season." She tapped the letter that had started the whole conversation. "Since I'd never allow *American* werewolves to darken our door, I was thinking of something grander. England. Some of those British monsters are even titled."

Faith couldn't face the potato. She slid it off her fork untouched. *Not more society. Critical eyes, and uncomfortable clothes, mixed with monsters.* The potato wobbled. Imagine having to sit across the table from a real vampire. Those fangs. *Do they suck blood at dinner?* She shuddered.

Mrs Wigglesworth continued, "Then she might marry and stay across the ocean."

"To rot," added Faith under her breath. The subtext being that then the Wigglesworths would never have to see their youngest daughter again.

Her mother gave a tight smile. "Cursing some monster with her wicked ways and amoral behavior, instead of us and our good name."

Faith tried not to find that funny. *Isn't that what they call the irresistible need to shapeshift every full moon – werewolf's curse? Midnight special,* she thought, *curse now comes with your very own indiscreet American fortune hunter. Buy while fresh.*

Papa made his decision. "Send her to England then, my dear. No one will have heard of her shame there."

No one will have heard of me at all. Faith was cheered by that thought. *Oh, the joy of anonymity.*

"Hardly matters. Werewolves don't have standards." Mrs Wigglesworth spoke with unsubstantiated confidence.

Faith actually didn't mind overmuch. Anything to get out of the house. Apparently, she hadn't any standards either.

Her mother glared at her, sharp and vicious. "We are being whispered about. In the streets! Mrs Kensington cut me in the park yesterday. Me! I want you gone from here and forgotten. You will find yourself a werewolf, girl. You aren't good enough for a human man. Not even an English one."

Faith hung her head. *She wants me shamed for the rest of my life. Tied forever to the same supernatural creatures that deceived and ruined me. All because she is being whispered about this month in a minor scandal that will be forgotten by summer.*

So it was that Faith, with only her maid Minnie as

chaperone, and last season's dresses (which might themselves be considered a chaperone, for the discouragement that they afforded) and a few outfits Faith had made in secret (even more discouraging to prospective suitors, as these involved menswear), were packed into a dirigible and floated off to England. Properly, Mrs Wigglesworth ought to have gone along, but Faith's mother obviously thought nothing worse could happen to her daughter.

She was, of course, entirely wrong.

Faith enjoyed the Atlantic crossing. Their dirigible, the *Flotty*, was a spacious, comfortable craft with amiable staff and excellent south-facing aspects. Their room was underdone, like raw pastry – damp and cool and unfinished – but Faith suspected her parents of penny-pinching in that regard and did not blame the ship. Poor Minnie was airsick the entire passage, but Faith was a strong floater with a head for heights. She spent most of her time abovedecks, enjoying the peaceful grey of the aetheric void. The prevailing cotton-wooly numbness suited her mood perfectly. Looking into the aether was like looking into her own soul – an empty void. She enjoyed it. It suited her to delve into a funk.

"Miss, you shouldn't allow yourself to be maudlin." Minnie roused herself enough to be critical when Faith came in one evening to change before a meal.

"Why shouldn't I be maudlin? If anyone has the right, it's me."

"Now, miss, you've resisted it so far."

"That was before they packed me off to England to catch myself a wolf."

"Could be worse fates," said Minnie.

"Oh, yes?"

"Could have airsickness like me." Minnie was turning green again even as they spoke.

"Yes, you're right, poor dear. More cold cloths? Could you manage a little barley water?"

Minnie clutched her tummy and moaned at the very idea of barley water, reaching for a bucket.

Faith made a hasty retreat in search of cold cloths and ginger nubbins.

They landed in London three days later, two hours after sunset. The city was beautiful, all lit up by gas lanterns, with other airships drifting about through halfhearted clouds. The moon was a slim crescent low on the horizon.

"I thought it was supposed to be a dirty, grungy place." Minnie had finally made it up onto the squeak deck for the depuffing.

Faith frowned down at their new home. "It seems nice enough."

Minnie did not look convinced.

They could see the Hyde Park embarkation green now, well lit to guide in the long-haul transports puffing in at night. She thought the park was probably pretty during the day, and much bigger than she'd anticipated.

Minnie glared at her mistress and not the view. "Will you be changing, miss?" Her tone suggested that Faith's outfit deserved nothing but censure.

Faith firmed her resolve. "I will not."

"Oh, miss." Minnie looked ill once more.

Their dirigible depuffed in stages. Minnie, while

green, managed to maintain her dignity as the *Flotty* sunk with all dignified gravitas.

Once all the way down, the gangplank lowered, and porters swarmed up it. Minnie instantly commandeered one for their luggage. Faith trailed dutifully after.

Major Channing Channing of the Chesterfield Channings crossed his arms over his not-insignificant chest and growled. Since he was usually growling about something, most of his field agents ignored both noise and stance. Some of the newer ones moved a little faster about their assigned tasks, glancing at him sideways. He only sneered at them.

It wasn't that they were being particularly incompetent. Nor that the mission was going any less slowly than expected. Just that Major Channing liked to growl. Being a werewolf, it was somewhat expected of him.

He was not excited about having to board and search this incoming dirigible. He wasn't confident in their information, Americans were innately untrustworthy, and the airship was also American make, registry, and crew, so it wouldn't be easy to investigate without giving offense.

But it must be done.

Reports indicated a shipment of Sundowner bullets was aboard, sent to arm the London Separatist movement and facilitate their anarchical agenda. Channing's agents in America had tracked the bullets to Boston, but there the trail went cold. It was only supposition that they were headed to London. Certainly, the Bostonians could make good use of such an armament themselves, America being a generally hostile place where immortals were concerned.

In England, such bullets were controlled and licensed strictly to Sundowners – those few people authorized to kill vampires and werewolves. More importantly, they were extremely expensive to produce. Channing was motivated to find them. Firstly, to keep them out of enemy hands, and secondly, so that he might restock his own supplies.

As the head of BUR, Channing was a licensed Sundowner himself. The possibility of new bullets was extremely tempting. Channing liked killing things, even his fellow immortals. *Especially them, more of a challenge. After all, everyone needs a hobby.*

Unfortunately, in this instance Channing was anticipating failure. And no killing. He had a feeling the bullets weren't on this dirigible, or if they were, they'd be too well hidden to discover without giving unpardonable offense to passengers through confiscation. This was one instance where even a werewolf's nose could be fooled, and BUR had, of course, no idea what the enemy looked like.

Major Channing was always one to gather as much information as possible before codifying a mission; forewarned was forearmed, as the saying went. In this case there wasn't enough to be going in with, and it was less four-armed than three-legged.

His men, three of them, all human, moved to stand next to the gangplank as the dirigible depuffed to ground. They looked with fierce assessing eyes at the debarking passengers. Transport vessel *Floatsome Jetsome*

Comefloatington, or *Flotty* for short, was heavy with humans and baggage. The porters had their work cut out for them.

Come for the season, no doubt. Channing grimaced in disgust.

London had seen an influx recently of American upstarts on the British marriage mart, most of them interested in the cachet of a title. Brash young women desperate to find an Englishman with conservative political leanings to match their own upbringing. They saw it, in part, as missionary work. Americans supplied females full of wholesome ideals and strong anti-supernatural values (and, of course, money) to the upper crust of London's high society. It was as if the colonies were returning home to save the British from themselves and the monsters they had become.

Channing's lip curled despite his best efforts.

He couldn't abide Americans.

Fritz-Lloyd Kerr, one of his newer agents, focused on a young lady, her maid, and their porter. The porter was struggling to load what looked to be a leather attaché case that had tumbled off the stacked baggage. The maid nipped in to rescue a wobbling sewing box while the porter hoisted the case back onto the pile. It was clearly much heavier than it ought to be.

Of course, one's mind went instantly to bullets.

Mr Kerr approached. "Miss, pardon the intrusion, but we are investigating an issue of contraband. May I examine the contents of that case, please?"

His tone made it clear this was not a request but a demand.

The young lady, a pretty little blonde chit in something that looked more like a bicycling outfit than a traveling gown, bristled and blushed at the same time. "No, you can't!"

Channing winced. *That accent. So harsh. Pity, coming from such a prettily shaped mouth.*

"I am afraid I must insist, miss." Mr Kerr was firm. Channing approved.

"Under what authority?" The American female was firm right back.

Mr Kerr reached into his waistcoat pocket and produced his license. "BUR, miss. Name's Kerr."

"And what, Mr Kerr, is this BUR that you represent?"

"The Bureau of Unnatural Registry, miss."

She jerked away at that, blue eyes wide in shock, glancing from Kerr to the other agents to Major Channing. Her maid gave a small gasp of horror.

Channing didn't move under their panicked regard, arms crossed firmly, making it clear he was in charge.

"Supernaturals?" the American girl squeaked. "Are you…" She trailed off, clearly upset.

Now it was Kerr's turn to blush. "No, miss." But he did slide his eyes over to Channing.

Stupid man. He should control his reactions better than that! Channing frowned. Mr Kerr would have to go back in for more training. He clearly wasn't yet ready for fieldwork when faced with an attractive blonde.

The young lady followed Kerr's gaze and her eyes went, if possible, even wider. Her blush deepened in color. Flustered, she seemed so vulnerable, and as a result quite tasty, which only served to irritate Channing further. The wolf in him wanted to hunt.

He marched over. Without saying anything, he confiscated the leather case in contention. It was indeed suspiciously heavy.

The girl, as it transpired, was no milk-water miss. He should have known that by the fact that she was apparently attired in... *Is that a split skirt or trousers? What are the young women wearing these days? Or perhaps it's simply a plague of the colonies.*

"Stop! That's mine. Don't you dare. Don't touch it!" So much for her being flustered.

She followed her case, unafraid of Channing.

That is rather novel.

She smelled wonderful, he realized dispassionately. Like port and mincemeat pie, at once both sweet and richly intoxicating.

Channing ignored her, rested the leather case on a folding card table he'd set up expressly for this purpose. Then he popped the lid open.

Now, what is she so desperate to hide?

Faith could not deny that the offensive gentleman was ridiculously handsome. So much so, it hurt to look at him. But he clearly knew well how effective his looks were. This served to mitigate any possible appeal. There was also no doubt in Faith's mind that he was a vampire. His slave (or drone, or whatever a servant was called) had indicated him as the immortal in charge of this harassment.

He wore no uniform, but he had the feel of arrogance and authority. Every line of his posture bespoke not only elevated breeding but military training. Instructions were barked at her in the manner of a militia captain or a French chef.

At the moment, he was silent and the muscles in his jaw rippled as he clenched his teeth.

Obviously a vampire. He had the pale skin she'd been told to expect. He was tall and lean and cut-glass pretty, blond and sharp-featured with too many teeth, like an ice sculpture wearing dentures.

He was also extraordinarily rude. To steal her specimen case without asking!

The first thing I do in a new country is subject myself to official humiliation. Oh, why did I insist on bringing my collection with me?

Faith knew why. Because her parents would have unceremoniously thrown it all away despite the fact that it was the work of years. Faith had begun collecting when she was only ten. Her mother had prayed she'd grow out of the obsession, but Faith never did. Faith intended to keep collecting until she died, despite the embarrassment of such an unwomanly hobby. Her collecting missions were exciting without too much risk. She found the associated cataloging afterwards restful, and the scholarly papers that resulted? Well, they were very well received in *certain* circles, thank you very much. Although published under a male pseudonym.

Of course, it was not the kind of hobby a young lady was supposed to cultivate. Botany, particularly botanical sketching, was about as far as respectable women were supposed to go into the natural sciences.

Not rocks. Never rocks.

Faith bit her lip and knew she was blushing. For the gorgeous vampire was about to expose her sins to the world. Or at least the small corner of it in Hyde Park that evening.

He lifted the lid for her case and then removed the

thick woolen shawl she'd tucked in to seal the top. The case was velvet-lined, unnecessary, and subdivided into squares, necessary. It held several shelves stacked atop each other, so that the one could be lifted out to show the next underneath like a very large and very sturdy jewelry box or small treasure chest.

Faith was proud of the design. She'd commissioned it herself with carefully hoarded pin money. Her mother was exasperated upon discovering the unnecessary expense. *Why not buy some new fans, child? Fans are so much more useful to a girl.*

This was before *the incident,* when Mrs Wigglesworth was more tolerant of Faith's eccentricities. Before her indiscretion. Before her shame. Now her collection was just one more thing that made her unbearable to be around, a dishonor to the family.

Here I arrive in a foreign land, all prepared to do it right this time, or at least to try my level best, and already I'm failing.

The vampire lifted out the first shelf. And then the second. And then the third, and set them out on the table. His face had gone from suspicious and guarded to a certain blankness that might indicate surprise.

"Rocks." He spoke at last. His voice was somehow the most British-sounding thing ever. His vowels were all wet and round.

Faith moved closer and huffed at him. "Yes, sir. *Rocks.* Well, and a few minerals. Even a fossil or two. What did you think they were?"

"That" – his tone was sharp and curt – "is absolutely none of your concern. Why are you gallivanting about the aetherosphere with a ruddy great load of rocks?"

"No need to take that tone with me, sir!" Faith glared.

She shouldn't have to defend herself. After all, rocks weren't contraband. Not that she knew of, anyway.

Minnie, heretofore wide-eyed and terrified, recognized Faith's tone and plucked up enough courage to say, "Now, miss, don't be hasty."

Faith ignored her maid and put her hands on her hips. "Is there something *wrong* with my collection? Are the British opposed to the immigration of foreign rocks in principle or just in theory? Is there a standing law against the importation of stones?"

He looked nonplussed at her attack.

Faith gave him a small, pitying smile.

Minnie backed away, no doubt putting herself out of shrapnel distance.

Very little made Faith genuinely angry; she worked hard against it, what with her mother's irrational temper as a shining example of how *not* to behave. However, she would tolerate *no* criticism of her collection, not from geologically ignorant vampires!

"I assure you, sir, these rocks are mostly harmless. Your virtue is safe from nefarious rock infiltration. As, for that matter, is England's."

"Do you talk nonsense by habit, Miss – what is your name, by the way? – or is it an act of defiance?"

Faith drew herself up; two could play at this game. "I'm moved to absurdity when faced with unwarranted unpacking of my private possessions. I assure you, those are *my* rocks. I've collected them in good standing. I've records for each and every one. A few of the rarer specimens are even registered with my local chapter of the North Eastern Minerals Examination and Reportage Collective. And it's Miss None-of-your-business, *sir*."

The offensive gentleman picked up one of her more

precious pieces, a palm-sized deep blue rock with black and yellow striations. "What is this one?"

"Lapis lazuli, metamorphic, all the way from Colorado. It's pretty, isn't it? Oh, would you like me to prove my expertise?" Faith instantly lost some of her anger to the rush of information and pride in her own knowledge. "The main mineral is lazurite. It was highly prized in antiquity." She barreled on with a will. "Until recently, it was also used in oil painting and—"

"I'm sure it's most fascinating, miss."

"Yes, yes, it is. But I understand if you're too limited in your interests to share my passion. I understand you immortals lose your capacity for such foibles."

The man turned the lapis lazuli about in his hand, white fingers a startling contrast to the blue. His nails were very short and his skin looked smooth. "Are rocks a customary course of study for American girls of decent upbringing?" Either he'd given her split skirts a professional assessment and found the fabric acceptably expensive, or his use of the word *decent* was all sarcasm. Faith bristled. Cranberry taffeta might be considered a little loud for an unmarried lady, but her shirtwaist was wool plaid, which she felt toned it down considerably. No one could critique the logic of dress reform for floating; Faith hadn't even needed skirt tapes!

Faith was seized with the urge to be slightly evil. "You mean it isn't, in London?" She made her voice go breathy. "Geology is all the rage back home. Any lady worth her salt knows her minerals by rote."

"You are having me on." He did not sound amused.

Faith widened her eyes at him and tried to look innocent.

He fondled the lapis lazuli a moment longer. Then

said, sounding pained, "It is the color of your eyes."

Faith could only blink at that. She thought her eyes were not so dark a blue, but she would take the compliment, if that's what it was.

There was a commotion with one of the other BUR officers, or whatever they were called, that drew the much lighter blue gaze of the vampire away from Faith.

She thought she saw a moment of relief cross his perfect face.

"Oh, very well, take your rocks and be on your way, miss."

"I don't see that I need your permission. Good evening to you, sir." Faith began packing up the case herself, batting away the helpful hands of Mr Kerr, who seemed to feel some guilt over his part in waylaying her.

The vampire, whom Faith was beginning to suspect was also a scoundrel, said, grinning, "Welcome to London, Miss Lazuli."

STEP TWO

Situate Yourself in an Advantageous Location

Faith and her maid (and her rocks) made their way through the Customs House of Hyde Park dirigible embarkation green, which proved itself to be much less intrusive than their initial welcoming committee. Not quite as attractive, it must be admitted, but Faith preferred comfort over beauty. Or so she told herself.

She and her papers were given no more than a cursory glance. Apparently, customs officials felt that her walking suit passed muster as sufficiently respectable, for all that it sported divided skirts. *Take that, Mr Vampire-with-the-critical-eyes!*

Outside the customs house, the landing green resembled nothing so much as a countryside racetrack. Faith looked back at it, to see the tall blond figure of the vampire still messing around with her former airship and its personnel. She pitied the other passengers now facing his cool regard and patted her specimen case in a sympathetic manner.

She paused a moment to watch. He moved very gracefully for a big man, but then again, his was more a dancer's physique than a pugilist's. She found she preferred that in a man. In her limited experience (which had all been with werewolves), supernatural creatures were brutes. That vampire had seemed a pill, and considering his comment on her eyes, possibly a rake. But he didn't seem a brute. Although one never knew with immortals.

She looked around.

A large, flashy Isopod steam transport drew up. It was decidedly doodlebug-like in appearance but cheerful rather than creepy. It disgorged two ladies as alike in appearance, dress, and manners as to be twins, had the one not been twice the age of the other.

The younger of the two bustled over, approaching Faith with a sweet smile and eager step. Her face looked a little as if it had lost a bet with a chipmunk over the ability to stuff food into its cheeks, then got stuck. She had the rosy glow of the very robust or the overindulgent. Faith assumed, by her age (which was near Faith's own), that it was the former.

"Miss Wigglesworth?" the stranger said, eyes inquiring under a daring turban-style hat.

Faith smiled back, prepared to like this unknown cousin, who did not seem at all reluctant to meet her. *Maybe she has not learned of my disgrace.*

"Yes. Are you Miss Iftercast?" Faith offered her hand to shake.

The young lady (who might or might not be Miss Iftercast) looked at the proffered hand in confusion. Then suddenly brightened. "Oh, dear me, no, we don't do *that* here in London. No offense, of course, cultural differences and all that rot. Now, where were we? Oh, yes, I am indeed Miss Iftercast. Only, could we not do that bit? I mean to say I am jolly delighted to make your acquaintance at last, dearest cousin! I'm determined we shall be fast friends. Your given name is Faith, is it not? Tell me, may I call you Faith right away? It's such a lovely name."

Miss Iftercast had a pleasant breathy way of speaking and an accent only slightly less toothy and properly British than that of the unpleasant vampire. Faith was beginning to think this was the vocal styling of the uppermost crust of London society.

Faith, who hated her name, could not but respond to such warmth. It had been ages since anyone had actually been happy to see her. She was practically moved to tears. Especially after such an aggravating and embarrassing encounter over her rocks. Miss Iftercast had barely even glanced at the split skirts, either. It was a miracle welcome.

Faith marshaled her resources. "Feel free. And you are Theodora, I think. Yes?"

"Yes, I mean *no*. I mean to say, that's my proper name, but everyone calls me Teddy. And you simply *must* call me Teddy, too. Oh, I do adore your accent, it's divine."

"My accent? Oh, but it is you who have such a way of speaking vowels. So calming."

Teddy gave a tinkling laugh. "Mums says I'm too posh for words after they sent me to finishing school. And I said, well, what did they expect, wasting my time with elocution lessons when I could have been riding? I'm a great horse enthusiast, you see? And I can hunt like anything. Mums says I'm *too sporting by half* – overly horsey. Do you ride?"

Faith blinked under this diatribe. "Yes, I sure do.

Although I'm not as good as you, I suspect."

"That's quite all right, no one is." Teddy's grin took the bragging out of the words. "Daddy says I'm a *holy terror*. I'm always challenging my *beastly* brothers to race hither and thither, which of course I shouldn't now that I'm out and all grown up and on the marriage mart. I mean to say, what man would want a girl who can out-jump him at a mark?"

"A gentleman in possession of a large stable?" suggested Faith.

Teddy chuckled. "Oh, you are droll!"

Faith wished to make it clear from the start that she would hold her own, defend her friends, and be unswerving in her opinions. So, she added, "I think that any man who felt threatened because you could outride him is too fragile in his self-confidence to warrant a single second of your attention."

Teddy glowed. "Oh, we are going to get along splendidly! I've no sisters, you see. Surrounded by *beastly* brothers all my life. I cannot wait to have you stay with us. Charles is away on the Grand Tour, which will mean even numbers in the house at last!"

"Theodora, darling, sweetheart," called the voice of the older woman who could only be Mrs Iftercast. "Do bring our dear cousin along now. Do not keep her chatting out in the cold. She must be perfectly exhausted. All that horrible floating about."

Teddy whirled and linked her arm with Faith's. "Oh, how silly of me, so inconsiderate. You will learn soon enough that I am rather of an enthusiastic nature and I sometimes forget myself in my excitement. You seem more reserved. Or is that the shock of meeting me?" Teddy wore a dark brown velvet walking dress with embroidered daisies about the skirt and sleeves. She was much shorter than Faith, but bouncy with it. Sturdy and fit as opposed to slender. *Probably all that riding.* Her waist was trim, displayed admirably by a wide white sash. Or maybe that was an illusion made manifest by her sleeves, which were truly enormous. They brushed against Faith's elbow as they moved together towards the Isopod.

"I think you're adorable," said Faith, honestly.

Teddy beamed at her and then presented her to her mother. "Mums! This is Faith. She's a corker. I'll just go see the luggage stored and join you inside." She disappeared around the side of the conveyance with Minnie in her wake.

Faith's maid paused. "Should I rescue the case this time, miss?"

Faith shook her head. "No, thanks, Minnie. I'm sure it'll be fine now."

"Yes, miss."

Mrs Iftercast helped settle Faith inside the Isopod. It proved to be as flashy inside as out, with velvet-covered seats and the latest crank windows. Mrs Iftercast had the same open, friendly, rosy-cheeked visage as her daughter, only with wrinkles. Her hair was the same light brown, only with streaks of grey. He eyes were the same merry coffee color. She did not, however, seem to talk as much.

"How do you do, my dear? Welcome to London. Was your passage perfectly ghastly?"

Faith smiled and shook her head. "It was nice, actually. I like floating."

Mrs Iftercast shuddered. "Sooner you than me. Has my girl talked your ear off already? She is a terrible nuisance." This was said in tones of great affection.

"She's big on riding, I understand?"

"Horse-mad."

"We all have our interests. I myself collect rocks." Faith thought that, given what had so recently occurred, she should make this clear from the start.

Mrs Iftercast did not look at all shocked. "Do you indeed? How novel. Well, that, at least, you can keep under wraps. Theodora will insist, the moment an outing is suggested, that she ride, that she ride well, and that she challenge anyone willing to a race. Rocks, at least, are less arduous in public."

"I see what you mean. I don't need to mention them at all and I can collect in comparative privacy. Although occasionally, on a picnic, you may find me drifting about and pocketing a sample."

"There, you see? I can already tell you will be far less troublesome than my harridan of a daughter." Which answered that question. These distant relations clearly knew nothing of Faith's indiscretion, disgrace, and subsequent humiliation. The Atlantic was more vast than Faith had realized. Or these relations were much more distant.

Teddy rejoined them and Minnie climbed in behind her.

Faith asked, "How exactly are you related to me, again, Mrs Iftercast? Mother didn't say."

Mrs Iftercast frowned. "You know, I am not entirely certain. I believe your father is my husband's second or third cousin."

Teddy nodded. "Something like that." She tapped the ceiling of the conveyance with the handle of her parasol. "Steam on, James!"

The machine rumbled to life around them with a hissing sound so loud, it made conversation impossible, until moments later, they were humming through the park. Faith tried not to gawp out the window. *Land's sake,* she thought, *these relations of mine must be rich. What an impressive way to travel!*

Teddy asked, "Was the depuffing smooth? We have had these horrible winds lately."

"Very." Faith smiled at her. "Although there was something going on at the embarkation area when I landed. BUR was there. I think it's called BUR."

Teddy's eyes sparkled with interest. "They were investigating something nefarious? Oh, were they there to catch some malcontent? Was it a crime of some kind? A murder? An unsanctioned feeding, perhaps?"

Faith shook her head. "I don't think so. They were looking for some kind of object. They took my specimen case away from me, and opened it, and displayed the contents in front of everyone."

"Oh, how horrible! What an abysmal welcome for you, poor child. I shall write a sternly worded letter of complaint to the government as soon as we get home." Mrs Iftercast was clearly upset on Faith's behalf.

Faith blanched. "Please don't worry, cousin. It was just disconcerting. I think, well, I *believe*, that the gentleman who took my case was a *vampire*."

The two ladies perked up at that.

"Oh, really? I didn't think any of them could stretch their tether so far into Hyde Park." Teddy sucked her teeth in thought. "Unless it was a rove, of course. And they usually go to Rotten Row. Which one was it?"

Faith hadn't realized there were so few vampires in London that each would be known by name. Like the nobility. *How extraordinary!*

"Well, he was tall and blond and handsome, with pale blue eyes."

Teddy pounced. "Do I detect a *tendre*?"

Faith held up a horrified hand. "I describe with artistic objectivity, not interest. He was rude, and probably a rake, or something like."

"My dear girl," said Mrs Iftercast, "*all* vampires are rakes. That's what makes them so interesting. But I think you must be mistaken. There aren't many blonds amongst the old-blooded these days. Lord Akeldama, of course, but you would have a great deal more to say if it were him. Everybody does. Are you convinced he was a vampire?"

Faith frowned. "Well, I assumed. It was something one of his men did, sort of indicated he was a supernatural creature. He was so pale, and aware of his own importance, I figured that indicated vampire. I've never met one before, so I've no basis for comparison."

The Iftercasts looked at one another.

Teddy said to her mother, "Perhaps... do you think?"

"He *is* head of BUR these days. But if he were down at the green, supervising things *himself,* it must be a very important object they were looking for. Very important." Mrs Iftercast sounded serious and interested.

"You know the gentleman?" Faith probed.

Teddy grinned at her. "When you said *handsome,* did you mean so good-looking you slightly wished to die right then and there, or offer yourself in sacrifice, but also not at all, because he likely would kill you without flinching and he certainly, without a doubt, would ruin your reputation?"

Faith nodded. "Yes, that's about right."

"Eyes so cold, you suspect they may cause frostbite?"

"You *do* know him."

Mrs Iftercast rolled her own eyes. "Theodora dear, so poetic. Do I detect a new hobby? You should take up verse. It would be so much less trouble than riding."

"No, Mums. Horses forever! But even you must acknowledge his beauty."

"Everyone acknowledges it. That is partly what is wrong with the man." Mrs Iftercast waggled her head in exasperation.

"What's the rest of what's wrong with him?" asked Faith.

"He is a werewolf, dear, not a vampire."

"A werewolf? But he looked so..." Faith stuttered. "...so civilized."

"Civilized? Major Channing? My darling girl, he's more than civilized, he's practically a politician. But not for you, I'm afraid. Your mother mentioned she thought you might do for a werewolf, but that particular one is unacceptable. I don't see why you must set your cap at any of them, mind you, but if you insist, I will see what I can do for you. Ordinarily, werewolves prefer widows or spinsters, but you're so pretty, we might find a way around that inclination. But, dear, don't you want a family of your own?"

Faith felt a slight roaring in her ears. *I did. I did want one. Once.*

Mrs Iftercast was sensitive to her discomfort. She reached across and patted her knee. "Not to worry, cousin. I am certain you will do very well. London is lousy with werewolves these days. Several members of our London Pack are eminently eligible and quite stable. Although not Major Channing, dear. He is far too much of a bother."

"Major Channing." Faith rolled the name about her tongue. "I figured he might've been in the military once."

"All werewolves serve, my dear, did you not know? But the major served longer than most and likes his officer's rank. He is not active at the moment. The London Pack is remaindered out of the Guards right now because of their new Alpha. They gave Major Channing BUR to keep him occupied. He's a restless sort. There are different kinds of werewolves. Major Channing is not the marrying kind."

Faith didn't know if she was relieved by this fact or perturbed. She resolved to put the exasperating man out of her mind and enjoy her new situation. The Iftercasts seemed friendly and chatty and nice. The fact that she was in London to net herself a werewolf husband seemed to be accepted as perfectly appropriate. She herself seemed to be accepted as such.

Faith felt, for the first time in years, almost happy.

Major Channing returned home to his pack shortly before dawn. Falmouth House was comparatively quiet, the children were abed (yes, there were children now, much to Channing's continued annoyance). The rest of the pack were not yet returned from their various errands of business or pleasure. The clavigers were all gone to sleep. He'd missed the final meal of the evening, but he thought he might rustle up something out of the pantry if he were lucky and Cook was feeling generous.

He followed his nose and found a pork pie. On it was

pinned a note that read, *For tomorrow's supper, absolutely not to be eaten. This means you, Major!* He cut himself a generous slice and sneered at the note.

He smeared his helping with hot mustard and quite enjoyed his feed, huddled in the dark kitchen like a beggar in his own home.

The gloom suited his mood. He was disappointed that the search had proved fruitless. He was also discomfited by the young American and her blue eyes and direct address. The two had combined to make him rather grumpy. Not that this was particularly abnormal for him.

No one disturbed his wallowing. He thought he might even make it to his chambers without having to actually speak with anyone – pack, claviger, or staff. *I should return home at this hour more often.*

Unfortunately, his Alpha found him, heralded by the comforting scent of sandalwood and pomade.

"Channing, how are you this evening?"

Biffy was an odd kind of Alpha. Slender, with a fencer's physique and lacking the bulk and height endemic to most werewolves, let alone Alphas. He was impossibly stylish, or perhaps one might say *practically* impossibly stylish. Werewolves were not known for their elegance of attire, for obvious reasons. When one was prone to stripping and turning into a slavering beast, one did not, as rule, care to invest too much in one's clothing. Channing cared so little, for example, that he missed his days as a soldier, when his attire had been chosen for him.

Biffy was not like this at all. He cherished deeply held feelings on his outward presentation. He'd spent years creating a pomade strong enough to keep his unruly werewolf mop under control. Then he'd made a mint selling it on Bond Street with his face sketched on the jar labels. He was young; perhaps that accounted for a certain foppishness. Some might say too young. He was, after all, only twenty years or so a werewolf, and barely half a year as London Pack Alpha.

But Biffy was a strong Alpha; every wolf could feel that. The tug on Channing's tether was sure and steady. It grounded him in a way he hadn't felt in years. He was embarrassingly grateful for the relief and the surety of that connection. He was gruff with his Alpha because he was gruff with everyone, but also because he felt safe.

Biffy didn't seem to mind.

Channing had challenged Biffy, of course, when Biffy first seized control of the London Pack. It was Channing's right and his duty as pack Gamma to cry challenge. Biffy had neatly defeated him, without fuss or too much bloodshed, and taking long enough for it not to appear embarrassingly easy. Stylish even in battle. They were both content with the outcome.

Sandalio de Rabiffano might look like an unthreatening popinjay, dandified and inconsequential, but as a wolf, he was unbearably fast and freakishly strong. He'd struggled initially, of course. Too young to control such a large and powerful pack. There had been a time there when they'd all felt unmoored and lost. Their Alpha had doubted himself, and so he doubted them, and so the pack doubted themselves. But then their pack Beta, Professor Lyall, had returned home. And now all was peaceful and safe, even with two human toddlers roaming about the den. (Channing still wasn't sure how *that* had happened.)

It wasn't that Channing necessarily disliked children. He simply didn't like the memories they incurred.

Another life. Another time. He'd rather his past stayed where it belonged, drowned by the weight of decades.

Biffy sat down across the kitchen table from him and watched him eat his pie.

Channing did not offer him any.

"How'd the Sundowner investigation go?" Biffy was careful not to touch the tabletop for fear of flour smudges on his lovely grey suit.

"How do you always know BUR business, Alpha? Sometimes I think you know it before I do, and I'm the head of the division."

"You know my training. I maintain many of my connections… from before. You know I don't like things messy. I don't like to be confused or uninformed." Strumming under Biffy's confession was Alpha possession and Alpha control. *My city,* the tether said to Channing. *My people. My responsibility.*

In his other life, Biffy had trained as a spy under the greatest vampire intelligencer of them all. But that was before his metamorphosis. He didn't work for the vampires anymore but he still craved information. The blood-suckers had instilled in him a desire that his mortal death had not cured. Biffy liked knowing what was going on in London. And in the world. He *needed* to know things. Recently, he'd begun training the pack to gather such knowledge for him. Of course, he already had Riehard, who was one of the best. But Biffy also had other contacts. No doubt one of them was at BUR.

"I should clean up my offices," said Channing.

"You know it wouldn't be effective."

It annoyed Channing to no end when Biffy did that. Channing would tell his Alpha about his job, if asked. But Biffy never asked for details on BUR operations. He searched things out using more secretive means. He also never asked Channing for his loyalty. *It's almost as if he thinks I've none left to give. Perhaps he is right.*

Channing gave his Alpha the information anyway; it was all he had to offer. "Trail turned cold in Hyde Park earlier this evening. I suspect the contraband never left Boston."

"Pity. You could have used a fresh supply."

Channing inclined his head but didn't answer, because he was chewing.

Biffy leaned back in his chair and narrowed his eyes slightly. "Something else happened, didn't it? In the park tonight."

"Did it?"

"I felt you waver."

"Did you? I didn't think we were so intimate that you could sniff out my feelings at a distance like that."

"A tether is a tether, Channing. You cannot fool me with that icy facade. You hurt deeper and harder than any of the others, so I feel you pulling at me the most."

"Do I? Do you? I shall try to control myself better."

"I wish you wouldn't."

Channing laughed, cold and sharp, a burst of pain bleeding out of his mouth. "You've no idea what you're asking for, Alpha."

"No, I don't. But you keep it all so close, tight to yourself. That's not pack. That's loner behavior. It pulls and frays and aches. You're hurting yourself and you're hurting us. I don't want to lose you, Channing. You're a prat but you're *my* prat."

"Have you asked Lyall or the others? Do you know why?"

"I do. But it's not worth shutting yourself off from us

because of what she did."

"Pack may not be enough to hold me? Is that what you're saying?" Channing's greatest fear tore at his throat, making his voice ragged.

"No, but I think it's what you believe. You could let it go, you know? I'm strong enough now, even for you."

Channing finished his slice of pie and cocked his head at his pretty young Alpha. "You're a *child*."

Biffy cocked his head back. Wolflike, mirroring his movement – sympathetic, strong, and present. He did not rise to the bait.

Finally, the Alpha said, "It won't break me, Channing. If you let me take on some of it. If you let her go, just a little."

"It's not you I'm worried about."

"No, it isn't, is it? People think because you are cold that you feel nothing. When in fact, it's quite the opposite."

"Don't accuse me of being deep, Alpha. And stop meddling – you're like a gossipy grandmother. Now that you've established yourself, you want to see the rest of us tied down and subdued."

Biffy flashed his sweet smile. "I'd settle for seeing you happy."

"You are a confounded romantic."

"Guilty as charged. So, what happened to twinge our tether?"

"There was this irritating American." Channing had no idea why he confessed even that much. Sometimes, it was hard to hide from an Alpha.

"An American, was it? Pretty?"

Channing glowered at him and refused to elucidate further.

Biffy only nodded to himself in that irritating way he had. "Very pretty, I take it. Was she—" Suddenly, the Alpha's head went up, nostrils flaring.

Channing instantly tensed. What was it? Loner in their territory? Break in one of the others' tether? Attack? Battle?

The expression on his Alpha's face went from concerned sympathy to incandescent joy. "Lyall's home."

Channing snorted at him.

Moments later, Professor Lyall slid quietly into the room. One eyebrow rose in inquiry at the sight of Channing and his pork pie remnants chatting alone with the Alpha in an unlit kitchen.

"Channing, how are you this evening?" The Beta's nondescript face was carefully neutral, although there was something to his eyes that suggested he was actually amused to find them thus situated.

Channing pointed at Biffy. "Take him away, Randolph, do. He's getting nosy again."

Professor Lyall came up behind their Alpha and ran his fingers through the young man's dark brown hair. Biffy leaned into the caress, closing his eyes briefly like a contented cat.

Channing groaned. "Stop it. I just ate."

Biffy grinned. "You're only jealous."

Channing rolled his eyes, stood up in a huff that was only partly simulated, and stormed out of the room. *Jealous. Of course I'm jealous.* And it wasn't even the love, or the contentment, or the easy affection that drove a spike into what was left of Channing's heart. It was that he'd set himself on this path and had walked it with confidence for decades, chosen to be solitary, because it seemed easier and he was lazy and afraid. And now he was trapped.

A pair of blue eyes, like lapis, had shaken him out of it for one sharp moment. His Alpha had felt it, that tiny shift. That opening of the trap. And Channing wanted to escape – he *desperately* wanted escape. Except that the pain of the iron teeth holding him back was all he knew now, and he was a coward.

Get yourself together, Channing, old man, she's a bloody American. She is not for you. And you most certainly are not for her.

STEP THREE

If You Must Be Bait, Be Very Stylish Bait

Faith found the Iftercast household to be much like its mistress – comfortable, casually opulent, cheerful, and mildly forgetful. The town house was situated in a desirable location just off Grosvenor Square, substantial without being too showy. This, too, was like its mistress.

They kept fashionable hours, with breakfast at noon, morning calls paid in the early afternoon (confusingly), and other business conducted at night. Faith supposed it made sense for a society built around the presence of supernatural creatures. Vampires and werewolves, after all, only came out after sunset.

So it was that when Faith came down at an hour she thought unpardonably late, in a bicycling outfit she was certain would be met with disapproval, it was to find the family still at table. And her outfit entirely ignored.

Mr Iftercast was as dour and reserved as his wife was convivial. His most prevalent characteristics, so far as Faith could tell, being limited tolerance for the eccentricities of his female family members and a predilection for reading the newspaper at table.

He mostly grunted when asked a direct question, although he was perfectly civil to Faith. He flipped the corner of his paper down when his wife introduced them, and gave her a curt nod and an abrupt, "Miss Wigglesworth. Welcome."

Faith now understood how this man was related to her father.

The two younger sons, like Teddy, took after their mother in appearance and temperament. Faith wondered idly about the eldest, who was away touring Europe. The younger Iftercasts were both home from university for the season and would thus be acting as primary escorts around town for Faith and Teddy. This fact cheered Faith immensely, as the young gentlemen were jolly, amiable sorts and it would be no pain to dance with either of them on a regular basis.

While Mr Iftercast ignored them, the ladies of his household commenced scheming.

It was decided that the first order of business should be shopping. There were no significant balls of note for several days. Teddy insisted she *must* peruse Faith's wardrobe so they could make a list of necessities, and so she might ascertain if Faith's dresses were of a high enough caliber for London.

Dutifully, after the eggs (which were fried and a little runny) and the bacon (which was more like ham) and the tea (which was delicious), Faith took Teddy back to her room for a wardrobe assessment and exorcism.

With Minnie's assistance, they perused all Faith's gowns and accessories. She had packed only her very best options, but they were several seasons old and those were *Boston* seasons.

Faith started off on the defensive. "When it's possible,

as you can probably tell, Teddy, I like to wear bicycle outfits. I find them less restrictive."

"A latent adoption of dress reform?"

"Will it cause offense here in England?"

"Not so much in this day and age, but you cannot wear such a thing to a ball. Surely you accept that truth? I mean for travel, and sporting activities, even for walking, and certainly in the daylight. I think you'll find London is adapting, although such attire is more a matter for the middle classes. You may detrimentally impact your chances with the real toffs. I think a bicycle suit is generally accepted about town. But for dinners? Or balls? It won't do."

Faith nodded, reluctantly. If she were really to net herself a werewolf husband, she supposed she ought to look the part, at least some of the time.

Minnie donned her most placating manner. "There, you see, miss? It won't be so bad." Minnie would prefer her mistress dress more to the height of fashion and less for her own comfort and taste. But then, Minnie was skilled with a needle and liked to show off. When Faith had been thrown over by her family, Minnie had suffered nearly as badly for lack of attractive dresses handed down and ways to display her art. She'd once earned a pretty penny taking seamstress work on the side. When Faith fell from grace, so did a quarter of Minnie's earnings.

Teddy began looking through the few dresses Faith had packed, tutting away. "Pardon me for saying so, my dear, but these will not do! The sleeves and skirts are too narrow, especially on the ball gowns. So confining! No wonder you dislike them so. You might trade on a modest character, but do you *want* to come off as particularly pious or prudish? I shouldn't say it, but I must – you will look *mature* in these walking dresses." Teddy paused, considering. "Which could help to attract werewolves, but your ball gowns *must* be lighter in color. You are not that *old,* Faith! Why did your family send you with such dark fabrics, so ill-suited to your complexion? Your mother wishes you to succeed here, does she not?"

Faith said, simply, "My mother wishes me to marry a werewolf and never go back to Boston. Is that your definition of success?"

Teddy was suddenly sharper and less carefree. "Is it yours?"

"I'm not convinced of the efficaciousness of werewolves, but I'll admit that never returning to Boston has its appeal."

Teddy looked sad. "You do not enjoy the company of your close family?"

"I've caused them problems with my willfulness." *That is one way of putting it.*

Teddy shook her head and made a *mew* noise of sympathy. "Well, my mother is very accepting of the newer ideals of womanhood. I am even allowed to wear split skirts for riding the bicycle, although she has not yet come around to my giving over side saddle. You will not find us so restrictive in this household."

Faith was relieved. She dared not tell Teddy the real reason for her exile. It was too great a sin for any to ignore. Even Teddy. No one could be that generous of spirit. Faith could only hope that her shame wouldn't cross the Atlantic and taint these sweet people by association. Still, it was nice to know she would not be monitored and punished and reprimanded for acting in a manner that came naturally.

She confessed some smaller truths instead. "I don't know why I'm so independently minded. My sisters all boiled to the correct temperature. Four of them in respectable marriages, and me with my rocks and my split skirts and my refusal to marry the candidates presented. Maybe Mother thinks a werewolf could better control me. Then I'd stop embarrassing my family." *Any more than I already have.*

Teddy was shocked. "I could hardly countenance it, you are such a charming creature. Embarrass them indeed. Preposterous!"

So I, too, thought, once. Faith dipped her head. "So, I need some new dresses. Now, is my jewelry good enough? I haven't much. Mother doesn't believe unmarried girls should sparkle."

Teddy nodded. "It's the same here. Pearls, of course, but only a single strand. A velvet ribbon about the neck is very popular right now. Thin enough not to hide bite marks, of course. Unmarried girls don't call on vampires and must prove it."

They moved on to other accessories.

As she sorted through scarves and shawls, Teddy probed, not rudely, but simply in an effort to better understand Faith's position and character. "I thought Americans hated werewolves. We were always told your branch of the family was not politically allied with ours in the matter of supernatural acceptance. That was one of the reasons they emigrated."

"You're not wrong. The gloves will pass muster?"

Teddy examined Faith's glove box. "Pass muster? Oh, you mean prove acceptable? Yes, they should be sufficient. No one wears them only once anymore. Hats next?"

Minnie pulled out Faith's hatboxes and opened each with a flourish.

Teddy was not pleased. "Oh, these will not do at all. How many seasons old are they? They look as if they might have been worn by your mother at her coming out. No offense, my dear."

Faith was not upset. She knew her hats were awful. "I know what you mean."

Teddy's shopping list was getting longer and longer. Faith worried over money. Her parents had given her very little and only enough for one slim season. She was embarrassed to bring it up but felt she must curb her new friend's enthusiasm.

"Teddy, dear, I'm not able to fund a whole new wardrobe."

Teddy's face fell. "Oh, you poor darling, they do not care much about you, do they?"

Faith thought of her parents in their big house. Her mother's diamonds. Her father's pocket watches. Her sisters' debuts had been things of beauty. As indeed had hers. All new dresses, fans, and gloves (the same ones she had with her now). But that was years ago. Faith's coming to London was an act of desperation, not celebration.

"My parents have the ability but not the will." Faith kept her tone carefully neutral.

Teddy flushed in anger. Her pretty face showed all she felt without guile. "And all because you would not marry where they wished? This thing with the werewolves, they consider it a punishment, don't they?"

Faith nodded.

Teddy tilted her head. "Which is difficult for me to

comprehend, as here in London it is considered a very good match, especially for a widow. Was there something particular that caused them to insist on a supernatural approach?"

"Yes, but please don't ask. Maybe someday I'll tell you, but it's not easy for me."

Teddy touched Faith's hand. "Say nothing further, dearest cousin. I will get it out of you eventually, you know I shall. But I understand well that not everyone can chatter so ceaselessly as I." She grinned. "It's a gift. Although Daddy calls it the family curse. He is one of those not blessed with the capacity for easy conversation."

Faith said, on a hush, because she did not want to seem critical of her host, "I don't think I heard him string six words together during all of breakfast."

Teddy giggled. "I know, isn't he awful? Charles is *exactly* like him. We're so lucky to have Cyril and Colin as escorts this season. They're *awful,* of course, but fun about it. It's humiliating to always appear with one's brothers, but that won't harm your chances. Sadly, they don't run with the werewolves, being neither military nor political, but Mums will do her best for you. And Papa has some connections." She barely paused for breath, helping Minnie close up the hatboxes. "Now, given the state of your hats, I think we ought to go hat shopping first. You'll need something for the park tomorrow. Hat shopping should help with the werewolf problem as well. We shall donate these shabby specimens to the deserving poor. Although perhaps, they are more worthy of the *undeserving.*"

Minnie gasped but Faith laughed.

With which declaration, Teddy selected gloves and

the least offensive hat for Faith to wear out that evening, and dragged her down to the sitting room, leaving poor Minnie to clean up the chaos that had resulted.

Never in her life had Faith visited such a glorious hat shop. Really, it put all her shopping in general, prior to this exact moment, to shame.

Chapeau de Poupe was large, but not so large as to be off-putting. The hats were carefully curated and suspended via chains and ribbons from the ceiling. They swayed like wheat in the fields as patrons drifted through them. They were hung on the walls as well. There were attractive small displays scattered throughout, with gloves and fans, hair muffs and glassicals, and all manner of other necessities arranged atop.

It was after dark by the time they arrived (Mrs Iftercast taking nearly four hours to dress), and yet the hat shop was crowded, catering to ladies and their daughters preparing for the season. Or maybe their clientele was *supernatural*. Faith trembled only slightly at the thought. She was getting better at entertaining the possibility of supernatural ravishment. Or whatever it was they did that gave them such titillating reputations.

There was a vast hat selection. Faith was utterly overwhelmed by options. Always, before, her mother had chosen what was respectable and appropriate. For Faith to forage for herself was both a luxury and a burden. She would've looked to Teddy for help, except that her new friend was busy about her own desires. Besides, they clearly did not share a taste in hats. Teddy was attracted to extravagant, risky ventures that suited her round, rosy face and dark, defined features, but that would do nothing for Faith's more insipid coloring.

Mrs Iftercast seemed similarly minded to let Faith wander on her own, undisturbed. Or it was possible she had forgotten about her. Mrs Iftercast was overcome by enthusiastic adoration for a recent shipment of Italian straw. Faith ended up adrift in the sea of hats, helplessly drowning, as they all swayed around her at once.

Fortunately, she was rescued.

A young man approached. He was beautiful rather than handsome, with a smooth fairy quality to him that Faith would have guessed made him a dance instructor or an artist of some note.

"You look lost, miss. May I offer my assistance as navigator?"

"Sailing the sea of hats?"

"Indeed. I am Mr Rabiffano." He gave a tiny bow. "At your service."

He was an impossibly stylish gentleman – not a hair out of place. In addition to being impeccably well groomed, he wore a suit that was tailored perfectly to his lithe body. He had a milk-white complexion that would be the envy of young ladies, and pleasing contrasting dark brown hair and sympathetic blue eyes.

Faith thought at first he was brother or companion to one of the other shoppers, but as he showed her around, his consummate familiarity with the stock indicated he actually worked there. Surely, not merely a shop boy? Maybe the proprietor himself? Whatever the case, Faith was honored by his attention.

His taste was exquisite. He guided her towards small perches (*It would be a shame to cover those golden tresses*, he said). Faith settled on a beautiful straw confection with hawk feathers out the back and an apple-green velvet bow at the front. Mr Rabiffano (*Call me Biffy, do, everyone does*) said the color was perfection against her skin. He bypassed the season's more exaggerated offerings, all bows and ruffles and lace (*Too fussy for such a pretty face as yours*) and suggested simpler hats instead. He would set one upon her hair, sink into a trance-like reverie, and then shake his head without allowing her near a mirror. Finally, he stood and simply considered her (without a hat) thoughtfully.

"I wonder," he said.

Faith tilted her bare head at him. "Yes, sir?"

"You are, I think, an American?"

"What gave it away?" Faith joked, well aware that her accent left no one in any doubt.

"I wonder if I might persuade you to be rather daring."

"I have a feeling," said Faith without rancor, "that you might persuade me of pretty much anything, Mr Rabiffano."

"Biffy, please."

"Should I confess that I'm in possession of several bicycle ensembles and that I enjoy wearing split skirts and wide trousers on the regular?"

Biffy gleamed. "*You* are not afraid of risk! Most excellent." His blue eyes twinkling with glee, he led her towards a mirror near the back and seated her before it. "Wait here. I shall return in a moment."

Faith waited.

Teddy drifted over, dimples in evidence, wearing a monstrous orange peaked number with brown ribbon and yellow flowers all up one side. Faith thought it would look horrible on her, but Teddy carried it off, and it gave her some height. It would look better with that velvet dress from yesterday than the turban she had been wearing. Feeling they were on intimate enough terms for fashion honesty, Faith said as much. Teddy agreed.

"And how are you doing, cousin? I see his lordship has taken you in hand. You are lucky."

Faith quavered, "His lordship? You mean Biffy?"

Teddy nodded. "He is *wonderful,* isn't he?"

"Quite," said Faith, imitating her cousin's posh accent.

"Taken, though, or so the rumors go."

Faith was not crushed by this information. She had felt the young gentleman was being kind to her, but no more than kind. He was clearly not romantically intrigued. Besides, the man was prettier than she was.

"He's good with hats, then?"

Teddy pursed her lips. "The best. Only, I don't know what he is bringing to you now..." She trailed off.

Biffy returned, looking a little shifty, hands (and hat) tucked carefully behind his back.

He nodded to Teddy. "Miss Iftercast, is it not?"

"You remember, my lord!"

"I never forget a pretty face."

Teddy dimpled at him. "Or one who takes such risks as I do with hats? So you said. Do you see this one I have on?" She moved her head around coquettishly.

"It suits you admirably."

Teddy glowed with this approbation from the master. He turned to exchange glances with Faith in the mirror.

"Ready to be daring, Miss Wigglesworth?"

"I am strong and able." Faith smiled up at him.

"Close your eyes."

She felt the light weight of a hat upon her head.

"Open them."

She saw his grin in the mirror first; it was a wondrous thing, his approval warm and undemanding. Almost parental, which felt odd as he looked younger than she was. Then her eyes were drawn to the boater atop her head – a *gentleman's* boater. One of those flat, wide-brimmed straw numbers sported by young men rowing around a lake or on a picnic or watching cricket.

The entire hat shop fell silent.

Biffy bent to whisper in her ear. "They are being worn in Paris by young ladies of firm temperament. Forget, for a moment, its original intent and notice how well it suits your face? Perhaps with a blue ribbon, to match your eyes?"

Faith understood precisely his meaning. Against the background of all the frills and foibles of the other hats, the very simplicity of this one was glorious. The plain straw and wide brim suited her hair and face shape and made her eyes look huge. She liked the severity of it, the careful blankness. It was, as he had intimated, strangely daring.

"I love it," Faith pronounced, firmly. "It will go so well with my bicycle ensembles."

"Beautifully," agreed Biffy.

Faith caught his mischievousness. "Have you any other gentleman's hats that might suit a lady?"

"That's the spirit!" Biffy rubbed his hands together gleefully. "Let me ascertain. Of course, I am concerned by the size, but with hairstyles these days tending towards the poufy, and with a hat pin, I do not think it will be too much of an issue."

Teddy was gaping at her. "Oh, Faith, how wonderful. He intends to turn you into *an original!* This is most exciting."

Some twenty minutes later saw Faith at the counter with her apple-green perch and three additional hats, all originally intended for gentlemen. She had the lovely plain boater, a derby in pearl grey, and a riding hat of black silk. These last she would leave with Biffy, who said he would trim them slightly to make them a touch more feminine. Not too much, of course.

Faith was, however, still wearing the boater as she paid. She thought it looked remarkably well on her, and never before had she had such affection for a hat. She did not want to take it off until she must.

A familiar voice disturbed her transaction.

She whirled to find Major Channing standing behind her, a blank expression on his handsome face.

"Major Channing, what are you doing in a lady's hat shop?" Faith demanded before she could stop herself.

"Miss Lazuli? What are you doing in a *gentleman's hat?*" His cool blue eyes swept critically over her new acquisition.

It did not worry Faith; he was the type to be critical. If her new hat truly did offend, he would say something more pointed. "Mr Rabiffano will be trimming it for me. He wants me to start a new trend."

"He would."

A small silence ensued.

Finally, Faith broke it. "Now is the point where you explain your presence here, sir."

"I don't have to explain. We own the bally place."

"What on earth do you mean?"

"My pack owns this hat shop."

"You're telling me werewolves are the primary investors in a lady's hat concern? Don't you find this weird?"

"You have met my Alpha. I should think that explained everything."

Biffy wandered up at that juncture. "Miss Wigglesworth, you're acquainted with Major Channing? How droll."

"Only in passing. He insulted my rocks."

Biffy raised both eyebrows and gave her figure a slightly scandalous once-over. "Did he indeed? That doesn't sound like Major Channing at all."

Faith giggled and took off the boater, handing it back to him. "This is charming. I can't wait to see it when you're done with it."

Channing watched their friendly exchange with narrowed eyes. "So, you are properly called Miss Wigglesworth, are you? I think I prefer Lazuli."

Biffy hid a smile. "Major Channing, how unlike you to have an opinion. Why Lazuli?"

"Have you noticed the color of her eyes?" The man positively grumbled.

Biffy's eyebrows went up. "Indeed I have. What is interesting is that apparently, so have you."

Channing seemed to recollect himself. He straightened his spine. "Miss Wigglesworth, allow me to present you to Mr Rabiffano—"

"We've met. As you can see, he's been helping me with hats."

Channing soldiered on. "Who is also Lord Falmouth, who is also Alpha of the London Pack. *My* Alpha."

Faith blinked at Biffy. As strange as it was to imagine Major Channing as a werewolf, it was even stranger to imagine nice Mr Rabiffano as one.

"You're joking."

Biffy laughed and adjusted a lock of her hair that had been disturbed by the hats. She enjoyed the attention. Behind her, Channing made a funny growling noise.

Biffy said, "He's quite serious. Channing never jests, but it is sweet of you to think so."

"It is?"

"Yes, darling girl."

Faith frowned. "I'm beginning to doubt everything I thought I knew about werewolves."

"It wouldn't be the first time America got it wrong," grumbled Major Channing.

Biffy spoke as though he hadn't. "Now, I shall send the finished hats 'round no later than tomorrow midnight. You will need them right away, I suspect. And be sure to pick your gowns with care. Keep the masculine silhouette in mind. I believe it will continue to do you proud. No so far as to affect full masculine dress, mind you. I don't think you run with *that* particular pack." He gave a funny glance between her and Major Channing, which Faith chose to ignore.

The blond werewolf shifted to stand close. Faith felt his presence prickle the hairs at the back of her neck.

Faith concentrated on paying attention to Biffy's recommendations. "I shall do everything you suggest, Alpha Rabiffano." *He's abnormally creative for a supernatural.* Faith wondered if it would be rude to ask how that happened.

"No, dear, let's stay with simply Biffy, please. With you, I genuinely prefer it."

"I'm honored, my lord."

"And will you be attending Lady Papworth-Walmsley's ball on Saturday?" Biffy bustled behind the counter for a moment, making a note on her hats and what needed to be done to them. It was bizarre to see an Alpha werewolf behave in such a manner. Or perhaps it wasn't bizarre, and those few werewolves Faith had met before had been the aberrations. Which meant all her family's rules and warnings were mere hyperbole.

Faith blushed to realize she was staring. She was aware that Channing had shifted even closer. She glanced at him out of the corner of her eyes. He was still glowering, mostly at Biffy.

She remembered she'd been asked a question about a ball. "I'm sorry, I don't know. I'm at my cousin's disposal."

"Mrs Iftercast?"

Faith nodded.

Biffy smiled. "I shall strongly hint that you and your cousins be invited. If you aren't already, of course. I wish to see what you dare in the manner of ball gowns, Miss Wigglesworth. And Major Channing is looking forward to the event, aren't you, Channing?"

Major Channing's lip curled.

Biffy gave his pack-mate a small, indulgent smile. "There will be dancing. I do love to dance, although I am no longer quite so good as I once was. Do you enjoy dancing, Miss Wigglesworth?"

"Faith," said Faith, since he had gifted her with his preferred name. After all, she had nothing to lose at this juncture. She was about to wear gentlemen's hats in public; why stand on ceremony with an Alpha werewolf?

"Faith? What a pretty name."

"I prefer Lazuli," muttered Major Channing.

Faith and Biffy ignored him.

"And yes" – Faith lowered her eyes – "I love dancing."

Biffy nodded. "Of course you do. And you will not lack for partners, I'll warrant."

Major Channing managed to look both disgruntled and uncomfortable.

"Then I look forward to seeing you there, my lord Biffy." Faith made good her escape.

Teddy and her mother were standing near the door, clutching their packages and watching the whole exchange with avid eyes.

"Oh," said Biffy as he bowed them out of the shop, "I have absolutely no doubt you will see both of us."

STEP FOUR

Take Every Opportunity To Dance

"What are you about, Alpha?" asked Channing ten minutes later, after they'd taken the ascension chamber down from the hidden door at the back of the hat shop.

Biffy was all innocence as they walked the underground passage to their full-moon dungeon. "Oh, dear me, Channing, did you not want to go to the Papworth-Walmsley ball?"

"I never want to go to balls."

"But you'll go to this one."

"You practically promised the chit that I would."

"And that's the only reason? I never knew you to have such a care for my good word. How very noble and pack-minded of you all of a sudden."

Silence.

"She's a pretty thing, isn't she?" Biffy pressed his advantage.

"For an American." Channing squinted at his Alpha, curious despite himself. "Why such marked attention? People will think you are interested in courting her."

Biffy laughed. "They will not. The *ton* may be

willfully ignorant, but its rumor mill is neither stupid nor ill informed. I do not pretend to an interest in women and never have. Romantically, of course."

"So, why single her out?"

Biffy shrugged. "I like her. Such charming forthright ways. She knows her own mind, I think. Rare in one so young."

"She collects rocks."

"Hence the name Lazuli." Biffy's tone implied he already knew of this quirk in Miss Wigglesworth's character.

Biffy said nothing for a long moment, only shuffled some paperwork on the desk he'd set up to one side of the dungeon. The rest of the cavernous space was fitted with massive, heavy cages, for full moon security and safety. London's safety, mind you, not the pack's.

A small, smug smile was on the Alpha's handsome face when he next looked up.

Channing swallowed nervously and tensed.

"You call her Lazuli as if it means something to you. That alone would be enough to warrant my interest and favor. But there is something in her, something strong and resilient, like those rocks of hers, I suppose. I should like to see you break yourself against it."

Channing snorted.

"You are ice, Channing. You only think you are strong."

Foolish Alpha, I know I am not. I am weak and afraid. But I also cannot bear the idea of her dancing with all those other men without me there to keep her safe. She might be strong, but I think, perhaps, she has already burdened herself with too much, to be so tough so young.

An official invitation to Lady Papworth-Walmsley's ball was waiting for the Iftercasts at breakfast. Mrs Iftercast was in ecstasies to be so singled out. She totally disturbed Mr Iftercast's newspaper perusal with her enthusiastic squawking.

"Oh, my dears, this is such an honor! I cannot believe it of you, Faith, to have attracted Lord Falmouth's notice. I mean, I *can* believe it, because you are such a lovely girl, but still. Of all the werewolves in London. He was not even on my list of possibilities. I thought he was firmly off the market."

Faith tried to rein in this supposition. "I don't really think that's his reason for orchestrating our invitation."

"Mums, we believe he is using our Faith here for a social coup." Teddy spoke around a mouthful of eggs.

Mrs Iftercast glared at her daughter. "Swallow, *then* speak, Theodora! I declare, sometimes I wonder what we paid that school for."

"Sorry, Mums." Teddy looked unrepentant.

Faith was amazed. Mrs Iftercast was so wonderfully even-tempered. Had Faith done such a thing at dinner, Mrs Wigglesworth would have yelled and then slapped her, hard.

Mrs Iftercast only rolled her eyes at her daughter. "You're hopeless."

Faith automatically tried to smooth things over, just in case there was a temper hiding in there somewhere. "Lord Falmouth wishes to see me do well in society. I believe he wishes to set me up as *an original*."

"And what is that, if not his singling you out?" Mrs

Iftercast looked satisfied and mercenary.

Teddy came to Faith's defence. "It is not courting behavior, Mums. Especially not for a werewolf. He is making her attractive to others – that's not the normal way of things. He has given her no gifts, nor does he seem particularly protective towards her."

"And how would you know the details of homo lupine courtship behaviors, Theodora?"

Teddy grinned. "That, Mums darling, is *exactly* what you paid that school for."

Mr Iftercast snapped his paper. "Good. Got my money's worth."

Mrs Iftercast considered. "You may be right, dears. Still, even the friendship of Lord Falmouth is no small thing, cousin. I believe the hats may be a bit too much, but if he recommends them, you cannot but wear them. And if invitations such as these are the result… Well, you will be set. You both will be set. Not only will you have first dibs on the London Pack, Faith dear – the Alpha's approval bears great weight with his pack, you know? – but you will have entree into the highest echelons of progressive society."

Mr Iftercast looked up from his paper at that.

Mrs Iftercast gave him a telling arch look. "Yes, dear, this could have a positive impact on your political career. Of course, I have already sent our acceptance of this invitation. But now we have much to do and little time to do it in. There are gowns to consider. Theodora, your Worth will have to do."

Teddy said by way of explanation to Faith, "I have this one Worth gown in cream silk with roses strewn about and such intricate lace you wouldn't *believe*. It's *divine*. I want to live in it."

"Worth?"

Teddy's eyes went very wide. "Oh, darling cousin, you have a great deal to learn. And I have much to teach you. Worth is—"

"Not now, Theodora." Mrs Iftercast interrupted what looked to be a long ode to some designer or another. She turned her attention back to her guest. "Faith, darling, Theodora tells me you have nothing that will do. We must find you a dressmaker immediately."

"More shopping?" said Faith, worried. The hats had been delivered, but she'd yet to devise any form of remuneration. Biffy had asked for nothing when he took her order. She understood London shops to run on account, but she dearly hoped her hosts were not paying for her purchases themselves. The Iftercasts were already being far too generous.

Unfortunately, more shopping was indeed called for.

Ball gowns, it turned out, were rather anticlimactic after hats. The Iftercasts had a modiste they used regularly, but when Faith relayed Biffy's strict instructions as to her style of dress, her cousins agreed their seamstress would not do.

"We must find you someone willing to take risks. A newer shop with a younger proprietress. A woman with a reputation to build rather than to maintain." Mrs Iftercast looked worried.

Fortunately, they found success at the third shop they tried. The modiste, a Miss Cordelia Honeybun, was quietly intrigued when told the parameters of Faith's new wardrobe, where previous seamstresses had been shocked or disgusted.

Because Miss Honeybun had no established name, her costs were also reasonable (to Faith's profound relief).

She was even more interested in the challenge, once she learned that Faith's style had been recommended by Lord Falmouth.

"They say he has his jaws around the pulse of fashion. The first werewolf ever to take an interest." Miss Honeybun's voice was as sweet as her name. "He is very forward-thinking, I believe. The *ton* has been abuzz since he took power."

Miss Honeybun clearly knew that her role as modiste carried with it a requirement for not inconsiderable gossip.

Faith nodded, while the woman pinned swathes of fabric about her. "I like him a lot."

"And have you met the rest of the London Pack?"

"Only Major Channing."

"His Gamma," explained Teddy, who was sitting nearby and watching the fitting with interest. "You're so lucky to be tall, Faith. I could never carry off such a severe style."

The ball gown Miss Honeybun was draping was based only loosely on a Parisian fashion plate Faith picked out. Faith had pointed and explained, "Like this, only without all the frills. Very simple, Grecian almost, shows the fabric to advantage." She'd fallen in love with a bolt of sea-green velvet, a mermaid color. Biffy had instructed her to *stick with spring shades only.* No pastels and nothing too dark. "Spring will do you proud, especially as it *is* spring."

Faith thought the color looked well with her fair skin and hair. Her eyes were always a little difficult, slightly too dark a blue for the rest of her – better suited to a brunette, her mother was prone to lamenting.

If Miss Honeybun had time, she would appliqué silver

and white flowers about the neck and the hem of Faith's gown. But the ball was only a few days away, and she would be rushed to even finish the basic dress in time.

"I could loan you Minnie," suggested Faith, hoping she did not offend either woman with the offer. Minnie had a keen eye for fashion, and Faith thought she might enjoy spending time in a seamstress's shop, as opposed to enduring her normal maid duties.

"Oh, what a good idea," said Teddy.

Minnie perked up from where she had been watching the fitting avidly. "I'd love it, miss!"

Miss Honeybun looked cautiously relieved. "Are you adept with a needle, girl?"

Minnie nodded. "Yes, ma'am."

Miss Honeybun's smile was tight-lipped, but not mean. "I cannot ask for more. Are you willing to leave her with me immediately, miss?"

"Minnie?" asked Faith.

"Yes, please, miss."

"Teddy, will I do without a maid for tonight?"

"I'll loan you Emeline for your hair if necessary."

Mrs Iftercast stood at that. "If that's settled? I think we had best get on, my dears. You'll need white gloves for that dress, Faith. Do you have opera-length?"

Faith nodded.

"Oh, good. I'm assuming you have dancing slippers? Yes? Good. Then we only require something for your hair and a ribbon for your neck. Miss Honeybun, can you whip up something to match or should we shop further?"

"I am a full-service concern, Madame, and with this one's help, all should be ready in time for your ball."

"You're terrific," praised Faith, because she was. Also, Miss Honeybun seemed to be bristling slightly at an assumed insult to her skills, and one did not want one's dressmaker in a snit.

It worked. Miss Honeybun blushed. "You haven't seen the finished product yet, miss."

"I have faith in you," said Faith, because she felt the woman needed it. And then: "Have fun, Minnie. Let me know how it goes and if you require anything, please."

"Yes, miss."

The big night had arrived and Mrs Iftercast was patently nervous on the way to the ball. With Faith's mother, this would have meant tiptoeing around her for fear of a slap or a cruel rebuke. But with Mrs Iftercast, it only manifested in the form of her talking nonstop in the Isopod. She issued instructions to her three children without pause for the entire quarter hour's drive. Faith imagined her as a small, round brigadier hell-bent on strategic attacks of virulent politeness.

"Theodora, do not talk overmuch of horses. You know horses and werewolves are not compatible. It might offend the supernatural guests."

"Yes, Mums."

"Cyril, please don't disappear immediately into the card room. You must dance at least once with your sister and once with Miss Wigglesworth. And check back as the evening progresses. I expect both my girls to have full dance cards, but you must do your duty to the family first, before you go gambling away the family's money."

"Yes, Mother."

"Colin, try not to bumble. You will keep bumbling

your Viennese waltz. Better not to undertake it at all than be a bumbler. And do not pay too frequent address to that young Miss Fernhough. She's too young. You both are."

"But Mother! Miss Fernhough is a *pip*."

"Such vulgar language! One dance and one dance only. Now, Faith dear…"

"Yes, cousin?"

"Of course, you look absolutely ravishing, but perhaps no mention of rocks right away?"

"Not a single sedimentary sequence shall pass my lips, I promise." Faith attempted to look grave.

"I don't know what that means, dear, but thank you. Now, are we ready?"

The Isopod hissed to a stop.

Papworth House was a large concern with a most excellent aspect and desirable address. Faith would have known all this as they trod up the stairs even if Mrs Iftercast hadn't seen fit to tell her of it at length.

They arrived fashionably late, although not so late as to have missed the receiving line.

It was one of the first prestigious events of the season, so everyone who was anyone was in attendance. Either Mrs Iftercast or Teddy constantly explained precedence in Faith's ear as they waited. Before they even gave over their wraps, Faith counted nearly a dozen explanations as to who else important was arriving alongside and who was who in the receiving line. Once through that hubbub and into the ballroom itself, it became a constant barrage of who was everyone and anyone of note.

There were major politicians, minor royalty, aristocrats of every ilk, acceptable gentry, leading members of the *ton*, the very wealthy (which included a few fellow Americans), and, of course, noted members of the supernatural set. Because the hosts were progressive, the bevy of musicians set to entertain were drones belonging to the Wimbledon Hive. There were some clearly theatrical young men sent to fill the numbers and dance with all the ladies, but whom Faith took note to avoid, because they were clavigers. Faith had mingled with clavigers before, much to her shame. She would not ruin her chances in London.

There was one solitary vampire, the stunning Lord Ambrose, about whom all in attendance were curious. The last few decades, he'd rarely left his hive, and to have stretched his tether so far as Papworth House was an honor for all concerned (and a sublime coup for the hostess).

Lastly, there were three members of the London Pack – its Alpha, its Beta, and, much to everyone's shock, its Gamma. Major Channing caused quite the stir, as he never attended social events and eschewed balls as if they conferred alongside the punch some plague only werewolves could catch. And he was not wearing gloves. At a ball!

Lady Papworth-Walmsley was in ecstasies. Teddy explained that hers would be the assembly to beat for the remainder of the season. So long as the evening went smoothly, of course.

"No doubt she is a little nervous to have werewolves *and* a vampire. It's known they rarely mingle well. But I suspect even an altercation could only add to her standing."

"Teddy! You are wicked. Do you think it likely?" Faith's eyes flicked between the vampire to one side of the room, and Biffy and his Beta (a nondescript sandy-haired gentleman) on the other.

Teddy scoffed. "With Lord Falmouth present? I think it highly *unlikely*. He is so civilized, especially with his Beta nearby. But Lord Ambrose is an unknown entity. Just look at him. There is a gentleman who could tempt any young lady into sin."

Faith could only agree. On an aesthetic level, Lord Ambrose formulated anyone's ideal of what a vampire ought to look like. He was tall, dark, and handsome with a pale, sardonic brow and sculpted lips. Even as she stared, he seemed to sense her regard, and his eyes, predatory and sharp, homed in upon her. He took in her dress and hair and then focused on her neck, white and exposed with only the narrow velvet ribbon to indicate she was not available for feeding. He looked like he wanted to lick his lips.

Faith only barely kept herself from flinching.

His eyes caught on something behind her, and he sneered and turned back to his conversation, expression just this side of insultingly bored.

"Lazuli," said a voice with which Faith was now unfortunately familiar.

Faith prepared for battle and turned to face a man equally as tall, with lips equally as shapely as those of Lord Ambrose, but with maybe too many teeth and eyes the opposite of dark and brooding. "Major Channing. How are you this evening?"

"Very well." He looked it too, his lanky form in perfectly executed evening wear. His blond hair was queued neatly back.

"I understand this is not your typical haunt, sir."

"Haunting? No. Hunting, yes. Would you like to dance?"

Faith fumbled with her chatelaine, searching for her

card.

"Now."

Faith offered up her hand, feeling, it must be admitted, a little overwhelmed by his presence and by his insistence. She shivered, thrilled.

This was what she'd always hoped for in a werewolf.

They had a simple waltz. His hand on her back was sure and cool and very strong. She could feel power in those fingers, that supernatural strength, not that he muscled her about the floor, but it colored all his actions with caution. He did not wish to hurt her.

"How goes *your* hunting, Miss Wigglesworth?"

"I've not gone hiking for rocks yet. Although I seem to have caught myself some hats."

He seemed to be trying not to smile. "That was not the hunting to which I referred."

"Isn't it gauche to talk of such things?"

"Look around you, my Lazuli, see all the matrons with their precious daughters? See how they bend and flutter. See how they circle in on prospects and targets. Hunting is Britain's favorite sport, especially amongst the ladies of the *ton*."

"And what are you hunting, Major?"

"Information."

"And you think you'll be successful at this particular assembly?"

"There are some interesting players in place."

"You refer, perhaps, to Lord Ambrose?"

"Things are always more interesting when a vampire is involved."

"There are probably many who say the same thing about werewolves."

"They are not quite the same thing." It was clearly

important to him that she understand this.

"So I've been told. Funny, but I originally thought you belonged to the fanged set when we first met, and yet I find you belong to the furballs instead."

"They thought so too, once. Werewolf suits me better."

"Does it? You don't seem the type to play well inside a pack."

"It is not often a choice." He gave a faint smile. "All this you have gathered on my character in the space of one conversation about rocks and another about hats? Or have you made enquiries about me in particular?"

Channing could not help but feel smug. Faith had looked into his character. She had asked about him. She was intrigued.

He preened.

She smelled wonderful.

Of course, he too had made enquiries. He could hardly help himself. Five days since he had seen her last. Five days was enough time to determine what London knew of Miss Wigglesworth, if not quite enough time to get word back from his American contacts.

What am I doing? Channing wondered, not for the first time, as he whirled the young American girl about the floor.

She was sweet and pliant in his arms, as if she did not mind being kept there, as if she did not mind there was violence underneath. Or perhaps she did not think of herself as prey. Or perhaps she was unaware of the sound her pulse made in his head and the delicious scent of her – raisins soaked in brandy, Madeira cake and custard.

"I enquired about you, too." He allowed his thumb to stroke against her back and soothe away the threat in his words.

Nevertheless, she jerked a fraction, although her steps remained sure and steady. She knew well how to dance, this one. *She has danced with dangerous men before.*

"And what have you discovered, Major?" Her brows arched, finely formed and a shade darker than her hair. He was beginning to find her accent charming, which worried him.

"There is some scandal to your presence here. Some reason you left Boston for London. Some purpose to your placing your pretty face and golden hair on our marriage mart instead of yours."

"I'm sent to catch a werewolf husband, Major Channing, that's it. Aren't you afraid of me?"

He couldn't stop a small chuckle at that. "Shouldn't you be afraid of me? I have ruined women for lesser reasons then a mercenary agenda."

"Have you really? You aren't hungry for a wife, then, Major?"

"That ship has sailed." *Way back, too far.* He felt the old ache then, and wondered if he had nursed it so much into a bitter memory that the few pleasant moments of that time were now entirely lost to him.

Miss Wigglesworth gave him an assessing look out of her remarkable blue eyes. "You're a libertine? How very unique." She gave a small fake yawn.

She was, in that heartbeat, so perfect and so pure and so very dangerous indeed that all he could do was frighten her away. "Have you been listening at keyholes,

Lazuli? I assure you, they have always been willing, even when I ask that they pretend otherwise."

She blushed deep pink at that – an appealing thing, the blood high under her cheeks, warm and subtle and alive. He wanted to delve into her, with teeth and body until she was ravaged and supine and wrecked and bleeding and *his*.

She did not, as he had expected, break away from him mid-step. The blush was there, to be sure, but she was made of sterner stuff. Any true innocent would be repulsed by the intent in his tone. A woman without experience would fear the implication of his preferences – the certain acknowledgment that there was wolf, nothing but wolf, underneath all his icy indifference. Faith was intrigued.

She tilted her head and looked hard at him, her lovely eyes flinty. "So, you're just a beast who enjoys the chase, nothing else?"

"Exactly so."

She threw it all at him. Like a piece of warm fresh meat, cut and dripping temptation, enough to make him salivate, to bait her trap. "You can't catch me."

The waltz ended.

Channing returned to his pack-mates wearing a faintly bemused expression. Only they would notice, however, as his customary veneer was firmly in place.

"That lovely little American just gave you the dirtiest look I have ever seen you receive. Bravo, Channing," said his Alpha.

"Oh, come now, Biffy. Surely I've had worse."

Professor Lyall looked quietly amused. "What did you say to her?"

"Nothing but the truth."

"Now, *that* I do not believe at all." Biffy sipped a small glass of port. "What advantage could the truth possibly serve?"

The Beta looked equally unimpressed. "Your truths are clearly upsetting to a lady of quality, Channing."

"What makes you think she is upset? I merely intimated that I know there is some scandal to her being here in our city."

Biffy looked at him full and sharp, the Alpha in his eyes, the pull strong on Channing's tether. "Don't do it, Gamma." A direct command.

Channing looked away, taking in the ball with all its undercurrents of need and hope and fear. It made him want to sneeze. He curled his lip instead; it was all so sad and tawdry, and had been done so very many times before.

His Alpha clarified the order. "Don't toy with her and ruin her simply for your own amusement."

"I assure you, Alpha, I am not amused." Channing allowed himself to drift away.

Behind him, he heard Biffy say to Lyall, "Should we warn her?"

"It might have a deleterious effect. You saw the way she looked at him."

"You're inclined to suspect she may take it as a challenge?"

"Or wish to save him from himself. It has happened before."

Biffy sighed. He must know that Channing was still

within hearing. Perhaps he wanted his opinion known. *The opinion of my Alpha. Does it matter so much? Probably.*

What Biffy said next, then, must be taken as criticism. "How many times has he taken revenge on a woman for the sins of a wife decades dead?"

Channing ached, knowing that he disappointed his Alpha.

Professor Lyall's voice was low. "I have lost count, but you can understand why."

"He must be exhausted by it."

"I have never known him to be otherwise."

Channing gave a sardonic chuckle. Lyall knew most of the particulars, and in his quiet way, the Beta understood more than many could. But Betas were not the type to nurse resentment and pain – quite the opposite – so Lyall utterly failed to understand Channing's behavior.

Channing's attention was caught then by Miss Wigglesworth's laugh. Something a young gentleman had said. A young gentleman who stood too close and was now leading her out onto the floor for a polka.

Channing glared at them both. Come to London to trap a werewolf, had she? Thought that she was the hunter, did she? Well, he would show her what it meant to be hunted.

STEP FIVE

Become the Social Butterfly He Wants to Catch

Faith was enjoying her evening, the looming presence of Major Channing notwithstanding. He seemed to swoop in at odd times, presenting her with a glass of punch or distracting her from her conversation by glowering fiercely. She noticed that if she paid any one gentlemen too much attention for too long a time, the major would make himself known. Then he would disappear and ignore her once more.

It was sublimely aggravating. Like being desired by a very large mosquito.

He did not ask her to dance a second time.

After several hours of this sporadically irritating attention, she realized that he was worrying at her, trying to flush her out of her den, as hounds would a fox. She would have none of it and put a concerted effort into enjoying herself and avoiding him.

"What is he about?" said Teddy, annoyed on Faith's behalf. "Mr Nightingale was going to ask you to dance, I know he was. And he has four thousand a year and an estate in Devonshire. He's a most advantageous match.

His family might not countenance an American, but if you continue to curry Lord Falmouth's favor, they might make an exception in your case for the supernatural alliance afforded by the association. The major cannot be genuine in his interest, can he? He never pays court. Why does he keep running them off like that?"

Faith found herself smiling. "Well, I'm fine with it. I don't think I'd make Mr Nightingale a very good wife."

Teddy was shocked enough to snap her fan closed and lean forward. "Cousin, you grossly undervalue yourself!"

No, I don't, thought Faith. *For while Mr Nightingale's family may rise above my lowly American state, they could never rise above my other deficiencies of womanhood.*

She dared not say it, but in his way, Major Channing was doing her a service. She had no desire to secure any mortal gentleman's full attention. She did not consider herself available to a wholesome, proper husband, no matter how kind his words or genuine his interest. She was, after all, soiled goods. No decent man should want her and she was not about to ruin any man's life with her affection. Werewolves were another matter.

But there were only the three werewolves present at the ball. Lord Falmouth was unavailable, and Major Channing was impossible, and Professor Lyall... well, Professor Lyall was interesting.

Faith danced one dance with the London Pack Beta. She found Professor Lyall relaxed and, if not overly scintillating like the Alpha, at least not cold and fierce, like the Gamma. In fact, the good professor was oddly restful and accommodating – for a predator.

He mentioned the major, but only insofar as to say, "I

should warn you of his nature, Miss Wigglesworth, but I suspect that is part of the appeal."

"I haven't any designs on Major Channing, I promise. Despite whatever he's said to you."

"That may not matter."

"I'll be careful."

"That may not matter either."

Faith wondered if she could make delicate enquiries after other members of his pack. After all, he should know of any suitable, well, *suitors* amongst the ranks. But she was frightened to be on the receiving end of one of his sardonically raised eyebrows.

Professor Lyall was overly enigmatic, but she ended up liking him. They talked of rocks (despite Mrs Iftercast's warning) and he had a scientist's appreciation for her enthusiasm. He himself was more interested in animal husbandry, although the moniker of *professor* was honorific rather than descriptive. While their particular intellectual pursuits did not intersect, their spirits of inquiry were well matched.

He left her, after their dance, feeling enriched for the brief encounter and somewhat saddened that it was not he who set her pulse racing. For if any werewolf were to make a fine husband, it would be Professor Lyall.

But while Faith had been given a task by her family, a match to make and future to secure, she had her own agenda. She would marry a werewolf if she must, but she knew enough to wish for something more than complacency in a match. There would be no children, no growing old together. Knowing this, Faith wanted what she was not supposed to want at all and should know even less about. She wanted what had nearly destroyed her.

She wanted passion.

Faith danced twice with Alpha Biffy, Lord Falmouth. He was a most excellent dancer, to the precise step and not beyond. Not very imaginative, but then, he couldn't be anymore. The last of his mortality had taken with it most of his creativity, or so most physicians believed. Only his lovely hats now remained. Nevertheless, she enjoyed his dancing. Biffy made her laugh with his pithy commentary on the gathering and did not mention Major Channing at all.

When their second dance was over, Major Channing came once more to loom next to her, saying nothing. Biffy bowed himself away with a knowing smile.

"Your Alpha doesn't seem very fierce," Faith commented at last, genuinely interested but also desperate for something to say. Of course, what she was really saying was, *I understand that he isn't for me. And I'm not for him. He's too much a dandy and not enough a danger.*

She tried not to sound at all disappointed.

"Fierce? No. He does not need to be. That is what I am for." Major Channing left her again, looking reassured by their brief exchange and a little smug.

Only one incident marred Faith's enjoyment of the festivities. It was heralded by a slight hush about the room. Faith raised her head to find her card seized without ceremony and signed by the vampire, Lord Ambrose. He gave her a nod and then drifted away, only for her to discover that he had demanded the dinner dance.

During the course of their subsequent reel, she was given cause to suspect he looked upon her *as* the dinner.

"You are quite the excitement of the evening, Miss

Wigglesworth." The vampire spoke gallantly as he led her into the pattern. He was very stiff in his movements.

"I assure you, sir, it's a big surprise to me, too."

"Is it indeed? I suspected it to be, in fact, by carefully crafted design. Lord Falmouth has taken an interest. Your attire reflects his taste and not inconsiderable influence. Do you deny it?"

"I'm honored by the smallest scrap of his attention."

"Yes, he has that effect. You know he could have been one of ours had Lord Akeldama not bungled his household management? Such a tragedy."

Faith thought of Biffy and the way he looked at his Beta with eyes that shone. "I think he's good where he is. And your comments to a stranger on the matter might be considered impertinent."

"*You* dare to reprimand *me* over a breach in etiquette, as though I were a schoolgirl?"

"You *are* gossiping like one," Faith snapped back, daring a cheeky smile.

Lord Ambrose started at that. A spider who thought he had caught her in his web, only to find the web itself shaken and disrupted.

He leaned in, too close but still the correct distance to whirl her around the floor. "You are a ripe and ready young thing. Bold. Is it the American upbringing?"

"Maybe." Faith thought it probably paid to be cautious with vampires.

His smile was both pointed and pointy.

Their reel ended, and Faith was profoundly grateful for the short and invigorating nature of a dance that prohibited too much intimate talk. Then she was horrified to remember that this was the dinner dance and he was shortly to find her a plate and keep her company while she ate.

Lord Ambrose led her from the floor. His touch was cold. He seemed some marble god of old somehow squeezed into the confines of polite society.

"I see why the werewolves like you." It might have been a compliment.

"Do you indeed?" said a mellow voice, all the more threatening for its calmness.

Major Channing was back. He moved in a delicate but firm motion, and Faith found herself neatly separated from the vampire. The werewolf now stood between her and Lord Ambrose.

Lord Ambrose hissed, surprised and snakelike. "That was the dinner dance."

"You signed for it without request. I watched you. Regardless, she is American. She knows not what she offers, to dance the repast reel with a vampire."

"Ignorance of social rules does not pardon her blunder."

"You're crabby because you're hungry. That does not change the fact that this one was my prey from the beginning." Channing's tone was beyond mocking.

Lord Ambrose looked highly affronted. "You cannot have a prior claim to this lady."

"I saw her first," answered Major Channing, sounding not unlike a child with his favorite toy.

"Never doubt, wolf, that we make the rules here. Have you offered her a claviger contract?"

"Stand down, blood-sucker." Channing sounded every inch the soldier.

Faith looked between the two posturing predators. "What about what *I* want?"

The two men looked at her, startled.

She turned to Lord Ambrose. "No thanks for my part, in either regard. I don't want to be your meal for the evening, nor your indentured drone for the year. I'm not creative, even if I were interested in metamorphosis. Which I'm not. Besides, as a woman, my chances of surviving a bite are tiny. Frankly, I don't like those odds and I find the idea of immortality off-putting. Although you honor me with your consideration."

She added that last bit because he was, after all, a vampire and an aristocrat. It wouldn't do to cause offense.

Channing grumbled. "He should have put it in writing."

Faith knew little about vampire drones and only slightly more about clavigers. She had once spent too much time with a claviger, but Kit had been cagey about the details of his service. She knew they provided daylight protection for their supernatural masters and that they worked to curry enough favor and show enough potential to be turned immortal. Vampire drones, Faith felt, probably had it worse, since they were also food.

Had Lord Ambrose's demanding the dinner dance meant something more significant than his fangs in her neck?

She gave Channing a questioning look.

He answered her. "It's not done simply to spout it out like that as a verbal insistence. The invitation to dine *on* you, I mean to say. And signing your dance card is underhanded. You know, Ambrose, that it won't hold up in court."

Lord Ambrose looked faintly embarrassed. "Well, you would go and get all territorial on me. Can't have that."

Channing arched a brow. "I am not interested in her as a claviger, either, my good man."

"No, I didn't really believe you were."

Channing snorted, leaned back, and crossed his arms. But he did not shift his protective stance between the two of them. Faith wondered how closely he'd watched them dancing.

She narrowed her eyes at him. "Do you always cause a scene, Major?"

"Always. It's why they don't let me out much. I'm badly mannered and indifferent to society's mores."

"He's a depraved old bounder. Why do you even pass the time of night with such a fellow, Miss Wigglesworth? A lady of refinement such as yourself." The vampire looked at her, but he did not expect an answer. It was all said to cut Major Channing down.

Faith grabbed the opening he had given her, nonetheless. "Honesty has its appeal."

"I very much doubt that. Especially in his case. You recognize his prior claim, then?"

Faith wished she fully understood the undercurrents here. But despite his aggravating ways, she felt safer throwing in her lot with Channing than Lord Ambrose. At least Channing came with a Biffy attachment. And while werewolves took wives, vampires did not. The blood-sucker's game was much deadlier and more permanent.

So, she said, "I do."

Major Channing's eyes went from cold chips of icy indifference to pale blue flames of victory.

Lord Ambrose gave a curt little bow to Faith and, ignoring the werewolf, left them both.

Major Channing looked down at her, once more cool

and contained. "He smells of rotten flesh and the long dead, and after that dance, so do you. I hate it."

Faith winced. "Well, it'll wear off eventually. It was a pretty short dance."

He grunted.

Faith was curious enough to be unguarded. "What do I normally smell like?"

"Plum pudding soaked in brandy," he answered promptly, "heady and rich with raisins."

"Raisins! I smell of booze and raisins? I…" Faith lost her words at that. She glared at Major Channing, who was looking amused by her show of temper.

"I believe I'll find my own way to supper, sir. Go away and pester someone else. Raisins indeed!"

Major Channing, mouth twitching with what could only be a repressed smile, drifted away, quite pleased with himself.

Faith's life became a whirlwind of entertainments and petty obligations after that. She and Teddy were the talk of the *ton*, to be found in most drawing rooms, paying calls and receiving them, and everything that came after.

The papers described Miss Wigglesworth as *effervescent yet sanguine* in a manner that was part insult, part admiration. *Brimming with American nerve*, they said. Faith decided to take this as a compliment. Apparently, half of London's eligible bachelors decided to take it as a ringing endorsement. Although it was possible they also thought she was wealthy. Americans had that reputation, too. Whatever the cause, the result was that the sitting room of the Iftercast house swelled with flowers from eager swains; there was even, unfortunately, some poetry.

"This one is an ode to my eyes, which are compared in one breath to sapphires which is then rhymed with camp-fires and in the next breath to fish eggs – which can't be complimentary." Faith put down the missive and looked at Teddy, who was red-faced in an effort not to laugh. "Can it?"

"I am certain he *means* to compliment."

"Well, then, the pen does him no favors." Faith, it must be said, was equally uninterested in the flowers. Botany, after all, was not her field of scientific focus.

Teddy, being Teddy, was pleased with her cousin's success and not nearly so envious as Faith dreaded she might be. Maybe it was in Teddy's nature to be generous of spirit, or maybe it was that one of the bouquets (a small modest one, containing mainly beautiful purple alfalfa flowers) was from young Mr Rafterwit. The sweetly bumbling Mr Rafterwit was a barrister of sufficient means to satisfy Mrs Iftercast, sufficient connections to satisfy Mr Iftercast, and sufficient horses to satisfy Teddy.

"He's very sporting." Teddy smiled over the purple blooms.

"Good, you won't get any poems."

"He keeps a stable of *twelve* horses in the country with a dear friend, for the purposes of breeding to race and to jump. He had a flyer in Ascot two years ago."

"And his character?" pressed Faith, because there was more to life than horses and pecuniary advances and connections, even if they came with alfalfa flowers.

"He's very quiet."

"Well, that should suit you."

"Oh?" Teddy laughed.

Faith blanched. "I didn't mean it like that!"

"Bah. I know I am a chatterbox. But I meant to imply that he is quiet when I meet with him. It is difficult – at a ball or even a dinner – to fully comprehend a gentleman's character, don't you find? I hardly feel I know him at all."

Faith nodded her agreement. It was challenging.

Throughout the course of the many balls and dinners over the past month, Faith had met and conversed with countless gentlemen. She had even met one or two more of the London Pack. Both proved to be large and charming, and were probably admirable prospective husbands for a soiled, if pretty, American with a substantial rock collection. Except, Faith did not feel she *knew* them at all. She certainly did not feel anything like the fire of personality that scorched her whenever she was in Major Channing's presence.

Of him, strangely, she knew a little. He did not even pretend to civility. Instead, he jumped directly into the meat of intimacy whenever they conversed, in a way Faith ought to have found shocking but instead found invigorating. She seemed unable to stop thinking about him and had come to crave their increasingly ridiculous banter.

"Why do you like rocks so much that you feel compelled to defiance and defence of them, my Lazuli?" He sat next to her at a supper party, eating raw liver from a cut-glass bowl while she sipped soup and tried not to splash.

Faith felt a little thrill at the possessiveness in the name. She willfully ignored it, of course, whenever he used it, but she liked that he'd given it to her – special. As if she mattered to him.

Faith had been conversing with Mr Koverswill, on her other side. Mr Koverswill had severe hair, pronounced ears, and an eye for trends. He'd told her (in confidence) that hair muffs were due for a resurgence. Faith had been moved to tap his wrist with her fan and tell him that the very idea was *hair-raising*. Mr Koverswill was utterly charmed by such forthright American wit. But then the hostess demanded his attention with some question about shawls, and Faith was left abandoned without conversation.

Channing had drawn her attention back to him, saving her from awkward silence with talk of geology. Not that he needed geology to get her attention. Faith always seemed oddly aware of him. Tonight, the moment he walked into the drawing room before dinner, the hairs on the back of her neck had tingled. Also, he tended to be near her if possible. She liked it, both his nearness and her awareness of it.

There was no question he would sit next to her at dinner. The hostess had arranged it and been smug about it. Everyone wanted to watch Major Channing attempt to court society's newly minted American sensation. Faith didn't mind. London's efforts to amuse itself at Channing's expense only increased the frequency of their encounters.

"Does hiking after specimens make you feel free of societal constraints?" His eyes were focused on hers and he seemed genuinely interested.

Faith was drawn into remembering her strolls about

the countryside back home, collecting and exploring, and her one trip westward under the liberty and vastness of the Colorado skies. She had always insisted that whenever her family traveled, they must stop in places they would ordinarily never consider except for her enthusiasm for the landscape. And then she must mitigate their exasperation at her continued delays.

She tried to explain her fascination. "Rocks represent so much time and space, so much history. Yet they're so solid and unchanging themselves."

"You are attracted to ancient things," he concluded.

I'm attracted to hard and sharp and immovable objects with predictable characteristics, she thought.

He regarded her closely. His eyes traced the memory of freckles on her nose, when she'd spent too much time exploring under the hot sun. Faded now. "We are not all so static as that. Some of us are sitting in the wrong time and place, even though we appear to walk about in this one. And some of us like change too much. We revel in the mayflies of life, for all we are stuck with mere existence ourselves."

He's telling me that he is not that kind of immortal. He's not a rock for me to collect. He's not steady and he'll not be constant.

She wondered why he was being so obvious in his interest if it wasn't genuine. She wondered if his intentions were honest. Was he chasing her in order to catch her or merely to keep others away? If he caught her, would he keep her? *And do I want that or am I also just enjoying the chase?*

Mr Koverswill returned his attention to her then. "Oh, Miss Wigglesworth, are you a lover of history of the ancient world as well? I have recently returned from

Rome."

"Italy? Was it everything you hoped?" Faith knew well how to keep a gentleman engaged. The young man puffed up under her regard. She felt Channing, on her other side, relax back in his seat, watchful.

Mr Koverswill put down his soup spoon. "A strange place. No supernatural creatures at all. No offence, Major Channing."

"None taken. You are wrong, of course."

"Am I indeed?"

Faith could not help but be surprised. "He is? I thought Italy was confirmed anti-supernatural."

"Merely because they do not like us does not mean we are not there. I visited recently myself."

Mr Koverswill cocked an eyebrow. "Indeed, sir."

Channing frowned; Faith wanted to reach out to smooth the lines off his forehead. "Perhaps not so recently – about twenty years ago."

"Were you there as a tourist, too?" Mr Koverswill asked.

"No. I was there to kill someone."

Mr Koverswill blanched.

Faith felt oddly proud. "What other reason could anyone have for visiting Italy?"

"And did you succeed?" Mr Koverswill asked, a tad injudiciously, Faith thought.

"Of course. Gave me terrible indigestion."

Faith giggled. She couldn't help it; poor Mr Koverswill's face was priceless. "You can't go around just eating Italians, Major. No matter what their belief system."

"Can you think of a better reason?"

Faith couldn't help it; she ought to focus again on Mr

Koverswill, but ribbing Channing was so much fun. "Never say you're an idealist, Major?"

"No, I simply don't condone mandates demanding species extermination. Especially not if it is my species."

"There, you see, Mr Koverswill?" said Faith in a desperate attempt not to keep ignoring the poor man. "It's nothing personal. Major Channing is just grumpy about his politics."

Channing laughed – a brief bark that was half surprise at his own amusement.

From across the table someone gasped, at which juncture Faith realized all attention was on them.

"Aren't we all, Miss Wigglesworth?" The hostess wore a pleased smile, her eyes glittering with appraisal. "Aren't we all?"

Miss Wigglesworth was described in the papers the next morning as *remarkably poised for her age, mistress of witty repartee, and capable of amusing even werewolves on occasion.*

Mr Koverswill sent 'round a beautiful bouquet of hothouse orchids.

"He has six thousand a year," said Teddy.

"Major Channing has been to Italy," said Faith, not really seeing the flowers.

Teddy, confused, agreed readily enough. "Yes, well, does that diminish his suit? He was in the army for a good long while, and Italy isn't that bad. Is it?"

Faith could see Channing as a soldier. He commanded easily, and he was cold and tough. "He hasn't sent me any flowers." This was more annoying than it should be. But also, she knew Channing would never want to be one of many. So, why would he send flowers?

"Do you think that has something to do with Italy?"

Faith giggled. "Oh, never mind Italy."

Teddy blinked at her. "I never have minded it. You're the one who brought it up."

"Where are we off to today?" Faith asked the most distracting thing she could think of.

"Oh! Well. There's a picnic..." And Teddy was off.

There was a picnic. It was outside in the full sun, so Major Channing could not join them. No werewolf could.

Faith missed him. She missed his presence, his constant challenge, the way he sometimes affected her breathing, and how she sometimes caught him watching the pulse at her throat.

She dressed with care that evening. Even though it was a gown she'd worn before, he hadn't yet seen her in it. She suspected he would be at the small private ball that night. Hostesses had started inviting him whenever they invited Faith. It was a kind of game amongst them.

The werewolf who'd once been nothing but absent from the social scene was becoming ubiquitous. But only if Miss Wigglesworth was also there. Now every hostess was eager to host the event at which the inevitable engagement was announced. It was true other men courted her, but her attention was nearly as marked as his.

Faith knew she ought to hide her regard. It was too bold. But the *ton* seemed disposed to humor her as confident as opposed to rash. And Faith had started to hope that Channing would not ruin her. That this werewolf could be trusted. That his intentions might even be honorable.

So, when he was at the ball that night and took the very first waltz, she let herself dream a little.

"Why will only a werewolf do?" he asked, as he twirled her expertly around the floor. "Are you frightened of true human affection, or is there something you find lacking in mortal men?"

It was a bold question, but Faith was tired of dissembling. She liked this too much. She liked him too much. "It is not something lacking in them so much as myself." She leaned into his impossible strength as if he might lift her up and spin her into flight.

"You are either falsely modest or sinfully devalued," he concluded.

I am exactly what I deserve to be, she thought. *And I will make the best of it.*

"My mother thinks a werewolf would be good for me."

"And you always do what your mother wishes?"

"Almost never, actually. I'm trying to be biddable for a change."

He chuckled and then sobered. "I don't think I'd be very good for you." He looked worn and sad.

"And why is that?" she wondered, no doubt surprising him with her American directness.

"Your eyes are so blue, my Lazuli," he said, looking into them, avoiding the question.

His were cold chips of ice. She thought of glaciers and how they carved through rock, and how ice had remade North America to its preferences. She considered the flat, barren plains that glaciers left behind, the fine till and the soft clay, and the wide emptiness of their absence.

I should like to be happy but I will settle for content, she concluded, wondering if this man with his cold eyes could give her either of those things. Wanting him anyway.

Around them, matrons watched and approved – another werewolf settled could only improve London's reputation. Mothers watched and regretted that they had not tried harder to secure Major Channing for their daughters, for who knew he could be such a gentleman? The occasional vampire shook his head at the state the country was coming to – really, an American? The occasional werewolf bit his lip and wondered, seeming afraid. Faith wasn't sure whether they were afraid for Channing or for her, the girl who clung to him and leaned back, so very trusting, feeling free in his arms.

He sent around a note the next morning, saying a scientist friend of his would provide her a letter of introduction to The Royal Geographic Society.

Was she interested?

Of course she was.

He added that there was a lecture next Thursday on local clay deposits and sedimentary formations.

Would she like to attend?

Of course she would.

She wrote back with evident delight in every stroke of her pen but added that her cousins would have to accompany her, as chaperone.

At the lecture that Thursday, they sat next to each other. Not touching but wanting to. She had no doubt that she confused him greatly with her obvious amusement when the lecturer referred to a paper written by a Mr Horner Carne.

I did not know my writing had made it across the pond.

"What amuses you so, Lazuli?" he whispered, away from Mrs Iftercast's hearing. "Do you know this Mr Carne?"

"In a manner of speaking." She was coy.

"You smell delicious," he replied.

Two days later saw them, once again, attending the same informal gathering. The kind that involved a hundred individually designed teacakes and a small circus performance. Faith had learned to be wary when the invitation said *informal gathering*.

"And how are you this evening, Mr Horner Carne?" he asked, drawing her into a corner of the room, while everyone else was playing parlor games. (The circus performers were now swilling sherry and bantering with the host over cards. Channing waved at one of them but did not stop to chat once he saw Faith.)

"You've found out my greatest secret," she teased. Not at all afraid he might expose her. He had nothing to gain from such a petty act.

"I must admit, I tried to read your papers and found them impossible to get through."

"They are dry, aren't they?"

"No! It was my ignorance, not your style. I could tell it was you from the tone of voice alone. I did not know geology could be so witty."

"And I did not know you could flatter with such tact."

"Only by accident," he admitted ruefully.

She threw her head back and laughed then, charmed by his disgruntlement. She noticed his icy gaze spark against her exposed neck and gloried in the thrum of awareness.

Heads turned at the joyful sound. The expressions were, mostly, approving. A few gentlemen looked disappointed. The young circus performer, whom Faith assumed must be a claviger to Channing's pack, stared at them with undisguised interest.

Faith stopped laughing and lowered her chin.

Channing's blue eyes returned to her face. "How goes the hunt? I have heard nothing from my pack on the matter of an engagement. Have you found yourself a nice loner with whom to flirt? They are not as stable as the rest of us, you know."

"Someone keeps interfering," she said sharply, more hurt at his asking than annoyed by his behavior. "Others are interested, but they're not werewolves. I'm set on this path and I'm not supposed to stray."

"Yes." His eyes were no longer on her but on the rest of the party, cautious, as though they were the enemy. "You want to please your mother."

Faith flinched. "Werewolves, I begin to suspect, are territorial." It was an accusation. *You tell the world I'm yours, but you don't make it so. No offer. No declaration.*

"It is true that none of my fellows will approach while I am here with you. But neither would any mortal gentleman. This is not because I am a werewolf, but because I am a scoundrel who has called men out for less. And that is not tied to my immortal nature, either, I assure you."

Faith was hurt by the implication of his indifference, so she was injudicious with her words. "Why must you ruin this for me? Your attention is too marked and my reputation will suffer." Faith knew she sounded plaintive, but she was also frightened. She was afraid he would take this as his opportunity to run. For all she resented his reluctance to commit, she craved his company.

"You believed it would be easy?" he scoffed, and she thought maybe he didn't even know himself why he felt compelled to pursue her. To seek her out.

He bent slowly, giving her time to flee. When she did not, he nuzzled her neck and tasted her there. Lightly and with only his lips, but she knew his teeth were eager and her pulse beat extra hard in an involuntary temptation.

"They keep sending me flowers," she said to distract him and to remind him that there were others interested. That they were not, in fact, alone at this moment.

"Do *they* indeed?" He did not look pleased to know he had competition. Maybe this really was nothing more than a game to him. Maybe he didn't think of her at all when they were apart.

Except that the next day he sent her rocks by special courier – a geode of purple to rival Teddy's now wilted alfalfa, and a growth of rose quartz, palm-sized and lustrous. She set the geode next to her bed and stroked it before falling asleep, as if it were a pet, or the head of a great white wolf.

She learned that night, when he never showed up at the theater, that Major Channing had left London on urgent business and no one knew when he would return.

London hostesses understood werewolf business obligations. And while they were not pleased at being denied the pleasure of a declaration, they still invited Faith and, by default, the Iftercasts to their gatherings. And Faith still went.

It was, oddly, lonely without him. She was surrounded by eager swains, fashionable gentlemen who wished to bask in the glow of London's favorite American, Lord Falmouth's *original*. Many a young man was eager to take advantage of Major Channing's absence. They were curious, too; what had such a werewolf seen in her? What about this girl had captured the attention of such a confirmed recalcitrant reprobate?

Faith did her best to meet social expectations. To be vivacious and sparkling even though she felt lackluster. Conversations with other men were so much more stilted, so much less intimate. She missed the way Channing held her when they danced together, slightly too close, slightly too hard – as if he could not stand to let her go. As if she could lean back in his embrace and they might spin and spin until they untethered from the earth and flew.

There was some speculation when he abandoned her without solidifying the deal. Had she lost him? Had he been toying with her and deluding them all? The *ton* did not like that possibility at all. So, naturally, it was *much* discussed.

Faith suspected that they would side with her if it came to light that he had played her false. It made her a little sick to even think of it. But London had adopted

Miss Wigglesworth, and they would not take kindly to Major Channing mistreating her. It was so much the opposite of Boston, it almost made her cry. That these strangers would give her the chance that had been withheld by her own people, by her own family.

Oddly, she felt a strange sympathy for Channing. Even as one week stretched to two and he remained away from her. Even as she doubted him. London was so very eager to blame him. To see Faith as the wronged party. They had probably doubted him from the start. They would not be surprised if he abandoned her, but they would not forgive him for it.

And yet, this is his home.

He is as mistrusted and as unwelcome here as I was in my mother's house.

It made Faith terribly sad for him, and angry at herself that she could not stifle her own compassion. Even as he stayed away from her. Even as it became evident that he would repeat the past. *Another werewolf betrayal.*

"Where have you been?" she asked, after three whole weeks without seeing him. Not even at the hat shop, and she had visited four times. *I missed you,* she felt, behind the words, and tried not to let that show. *And I own far too many hats now.* Thank goodness Biffy had taken to simply gifting them to her.

"Hunting deadly little creatures of American make."

"I'm not deadly."

"I was not hunting you."

"Did you catch them?"

"They are still at large."

Faith nodded, wondering if there was some connection to the embarrassing scene on the embarkation green when she'd first met him. Wondering that he could cut her off so completely. Wondering if this thing that was nothing between them had ended.

"Will I see you at the Brophys' ball?" she asked. But what she meant was *Are you letting me go?*

"I returned to town with nothing but that in mind." He was, as ever, all sarcasm and indifference, but his eyes were hot, as though he wanted to eat her up; she knew the truth in that moment. He wanted her very badly indeed. He had tried to stay away and failed.

I could have you, she thought. *If I wanted to try a real werewolf.*

"Will you save me a waltz?" There was something in his tone that suggested what he really meant was *Are* you *letting* me *go?* His eyes begged, even as they watched the pulse in her neck.

"You may have the dinner dance," she replied, and meant it this time. She knew exactly what was offering.

STEP SIX

Take Your Werewolf into The Garden for an Airing
They Must Be Exercised Regularly

Channing ruminated for a long time over the letter he'd just received from his contact in Boston. There was nothing new on the Sundowner bullets. He was beginning to think they had never existed at all. Except that his contact also said there was evidence of the manufacturer frantically searching for them.

So, they must never have arrived at their intended destination. Which meant they were somewhere loose in London, or somewhere loose in Boston. They really did exist – or why would anyone else be looking for them?

It was the second half of the letter that had him frowning, troubled over the contents.

He had asked, quite casually he thought, for his agent to look into the Wigglesworths.

The man was a consummate professional and, as such, assumed that this was BUR business. BUR meant supernatural and thus his information concerned the intersection between Faith's family and the supernatural set in Boston.

In New England, werewolves and vampires were barely tolerated and mostly ignored. They lived on the outskirts of society and did not influence or govern it as they did in England. After the American Civil War brought them out of the shadows to fight for the North, werewolves were granted citizenship and considered modestly acceptable in Yankee states, but remained utterly unwelcome south of the Mason-Dixon Line. Still, religious institutions throughout the states stood firm and rallied against them, and preachers held considerable sway over the American psyche.

The Wigglesworths, as it turned out, had had nothing to do with the local population of supernaturals. They'd also had very little to do with those who objected to their existence. At least until recently.

Staunch conservatives, the letter stated. *But not Sundowners and only active politically in the matter of anti-supernatural legislation. Faith's father was instrumental in passing a segregative act that prevents werewolves from entering the city of Boston except under escort. Ironic, considering they fought for the Union. His was the deciding vote.*

That was all he had to say except at the very last, where he had appended a note.

There is good evidence to suggest the youngest Wigglesworth, a daughter, was the victim of a calculated act of revenge on the part of a local werewolf pack. In response to her father's support of the above-mentioned act, the pack set a claviger to ruin her. He courted, bedded, and then declined to marry her – publicly.

Channing put down the missive, feeling sick. *Oh, my poor Lazuli, to be so humiliated. Being unmarriageable in her own country, they send her here to net a werewolf.*

Why? As an act of revenge? Her family thinks to punish us with her? What could possibly...

Marshaling his courage, Channing returned to the letter. His agent was blunt and to the point. *The young lady refused to cry rape, admitting to having been a willing partner.*

Channing felt a little like he might cry, for his brave girl had taken the blame, knowing it would destroy her. Probably, she also knew she had been set up from the start. How she must hate werewolves.

"Channing." His Alpha came into the library. "I must talk with you." Biffy caught Channing's expression then. "What's wrong? What has happened?"

"Another dead end," Channing answered, folding up the missive. "What did you need, Alpha?"

"You're being curt with the servants again. I know you won't do them actual violence, but—"

"I won't?"

"But they don't know that. And the clavigers are skittering about you on tiptoes, some of them literally since we secured that handsome ballet dancer to our den. You know we are short on clavigers. I can't have you being grumpy and running them off. I know navigating the social melee has you twitchy and upset, but could you please not take it out on them?"

Channing grunted.

Lyall gave a tiny cough at that juncture. *How did I miss him coming into the room as well? I must be distracted. What is this girl doing to me?*

"Sometimes, Professor, I doubt my own werewolf nature, for I did not see you there."

Lyall ignored this. "You are not usually this bad except when you're recently home from war."

"You've made a study of my temper over the decades?"

"Someone had to," muttered Biffy.

Lyall continued, a slight smile on his plain face. "You are one of those who struggle to leave battle behind and return to civilized life. Why do you think I have always tried, over the years, to be with you or to be there to welcome you home?"

Channing frowned. Thinking back to all his battles and wars – France, Spain, India, Africa, so many over the years. Lyall had indeed been there, mostly to step in and take a blow intended for another, or to divert his attention into a shift and fight, so he did not destroy those around him.

Channing winced – another flaw to add to his ever-growing list. "I was made in battle. It's difficult to abandon sometimes. That violence is part of me. I'm not certain how much of it is natural or supernatural anymore – wolf nature, Gamma position."

"And yet you miss fighting when you are home, do you not?" Biffy moved closer to him.

"Dealing out death is the only thing at which I am truly accomplished anymore." Channing thought the Alpha might touch him then. Channing wasn't certain if he wanted it or feared it, so he stood up from the desk and moved away from all possible sympathy.

He said, "BUR is keeping me occupied, and there is the occasional fight for honor or for pack. I visit the old regiment sometimes. But only a werewolf can really give me a challenge. In a good way, I mean."

Biffy and Lyall exchanged a look.

"There is another outlet," said Lyall at long last, with great circumspection.

"Some of the ladies down Albany Street are very accommodating to a wide range of tastes." Biffy was a great deal less circumspect.

Curse the pack for being a bunch of meddling gossips.

Channing curled a lip at him, which, with another Alpha or another topic of conversation, might be considered a challenge and grounds for discipline.

"And how, Alpha, would *you* ever know such a thing?"

Instead of taking offense, Biffy laughed. "I listen to the others talk about their light-skirts, for all I do not understand the inclination."

"Then perhaps you should have sent one of them to me with this well-meaning advice."

Biffy's eyes went hard. His voice turned ruthless. "Stop terrorizing the servants, Channing. I *don't care* how you get yourself out of this twitchy, angry mood you are in, but do it now. I believe I preferred you as a cold, elusive pollock."

Channing grinned. "Now you see why I work so hard for that state. Anything else is worse."

Biffy rolled his eyes. "You could try being happy. Or would that strain something?"

"He doesn't know how." Lyall's voice was sad.

Biffy glared at them both. "Oh, for goodness' sake, he's a werewolf, and he likes to fight. Is it so wrong to suggest he might, oh I don't know, fight for her?"

Then he stormed from the room.

Channing's jaw clenched as he watched his small Alpha march out.

"It hurts when he is disappointed in you, doesn't it?"

Channing's eyes flicked to his Beta. "This is no unusual occurrence. My Alphas over the decades are chronically disappointed in me. I have dealt with it before. He will get over it. They always do."

"It's not him I worry about."

"Never say you worry about me, Professor."

Lyall sighed and, instead of leaving, moved forwards to cock a hip against the desk. He fiddled for a moment with the letter that Channing had left folded there.

"Don't you dare read that." There was sharpness in Channing's voice, and the wolf lurked behind his eyes.

"You know me better than that." Lyall stilled and waited.

Channing lost his ire under Beta calm – imperceptible waves of patience that were also sublime strength. *What was I thinking? I know Lyall to be a man of principle. More so than I am, that's for certain. Also, I cannot take this Beta in a fight.*

When Channing shifted, he lost himself. He was all wolf instinct and violence. Oh, he was very strong, but he was also crazed. He forgot his human side to baser lusts. It was one of the reasons he could never be a loner. He might act the part, aloof and solitary, but he needed pack more than most.

Channing tilted his head back at Lyall, baring his throat.

"You will fix this thing that eats away at you, Channing," ordered Professor Lyall.

"It may not be up to me." The Brophys' ball was a positive squeeze, being both too popular and too packed, so that Faith wished she were anywhere but there. It was exhausting just trying to make one's way through the door.

She searched the gathering, trailing behind Teddy's determined push, from room to room. She could admit to herself that she was hunting for a blond head that stood a little higher than most others.

Teddy paused at the door to the music room. "I do declare, what a crush! Really, what possessed them to invite so many to a house decidedly insufficient to contain the number?"

"Teddy! They'll hear you."

"No one can hear *anything* in this noise. And how am I to find Mr Rafterwit in such a press? He said he would be here. He was going to tell me all about breeding stock."

"Teddy! Are you sure that's appropriate conversation for polite company?"

"Oh, Faith, don't be silly. His *horse* breeding stock, dear. Oh, you are droll! I imagine if I'm very lucky, I will be his breeding stock, so to speak, after our wedding and such."

"Teddy, really. Stop it."

Teddy grinned. "I'm quite looking forward to it. Oh, I know I shouldn't say such things, but there you have it. I think Barnaby is most awfully, well, *awfully*."

"It could be disappointing." Faith tried to put experience into her tone without actually sounding too experienced.

"Yes, but if that's the case, we won't have to do it too often, and Faith, you should see his horses! Oh, look, there he is!" Teddy waved madly at Mr Rafterwit; the poor man nodded shyly back.

Teddy charged across the room towards him.

Faith would have followed except she found herself neatly pulled aside by a firm, cool hand on her arm.

"Did you want that first dance now, Lazuli?"

"Major Channing, how nice to see you again so soon."

"Is it? Funny, but I think you actually mean that. You know, you are likely the only person in all of London who is ever happy to see me."

That made her sad, but she hid it with a soft smile.

He led her onto the floor, and then when the dance was done, he blatantly flouted the custom of relinquishing her arm to her next partner. Faith should not have been surprised; he had flouted the customary rules of conversation for weeks on end. Why should the rules of dancing be any different?

Instead of leading her back to her chaperone – where was Mrs Iftercast, anyway? Really, she was a tad bit forgetful and lax about her duties. (Not that Faith or Teddy minded the freedom this afforded them.) Instead of taking her respectably to the edge of the dance floor, where Faith's next admirer eagerly waited, Channing didn't even ask if she had one. And instead of offering to retrieve her punch or comestibles while she sat to catch her breath, Channing took her hand firmly and led her out of the ballroom and into the garden, where all was quiet and peaceful and they were alone.

Which was, of course, quite dangerous. But Faith found she could not be frightened and she did not care.

Channing dropped her hand and they walked together, silent and not touching, along an herbaceous border and across a manicured lawn into a copse of trees, ill tended and shrouded in shadows, at the very far end of the garden.

The perfect place, thought Faith, *for an assignation.*

Still, she found she did not care. She should have, for she knew better than most the risks a young lady took with a gentleman alone.

Then he said, "I know about the claviger. Your claviger."

And Faith's world shattered.

Channing heard her breath catch.

Her voice trembled only a little when she spoke. "He wasn't mine, not really. Never was and never would be. He belonged to the werewolves, and that, as it turned out, was all that counted."

"He made you feel as though he were yours, though, didn't he?"

"For a bit. Or maybe I just wanted the experience too much. Some moment of excitement. Some point in time where I was wanted without question. Maybe that's why I'm here with you now. Have you considered that?'

She was attacking, like a trapped animal, fierce and defensive.

Channing had decided to tell her he knew because he'd found out her secret and it wasn't his to keep. He hadn't been charged with this one, and he did not need another secret to burden his daylight sleep. He also wanted her to know that this was no grave thing, not to him. He *needed* her to know that. He would not judge and he would not reject her. He wasn't like them. He was a cad, but not in that way.

So, he phrased it the way he saw it. "He ruined you for his own amusement and showed you no mercy."

Faith had turned away and was looking back towards the house, through the trees and across the empty garden. "He did it because my father is an ass. And, frankly, my father *is* in fact an ass. I just never guessed his choices would burden me. I believe that the werewolves didn't mean to hurt me, not really. Frankly, I doubt they thought of me at all. They wanted to humiliate my parents. I was just collateral."

"Is that why you want to marry a werewolf? For revenge?" The sweet, intoxicating scent of her teased him with possibilities.

"No one else will have me, not if they find out," she said. "It's known that werewolves prefer a seasoned woman. Why else always go after widows?"

Channing laughed. "While it is true that purity is not valued by my compatriots, that is not why werewolves so often pursue widows."

Faith nodded. "You cannot have children, so you don't want to steal the opportunity away from a girl. And are you..." She paused, swallowing hard.

Despite himself, Channing found his eyes drawn to her beautiful white neck.

He wanted to lick it.

"Are you like your compatriots in this matter?"

He'd lost the thread of the conversation. "What?" he barked, sounding annoyed and trying not to.

"Do you value purity?"

"God's teeth, no. What right have I to that? I'm nothing if not impure myself. Why should I demand anything different in a lover? I mentioned my learning of your indiscretion not as a critique, Lazuli, but only so that you might know that I know. Between us, there is no need for secrecy in this matter."

"There's more." She trembled a little.

"And you may tell me if you wish, and I will listen and not judge, because who am I to judge? But only if you wish it, Lazuli."

"Not yet. That part hurts."

He hid a wince.

She sipped a small breath and soldiered on. "The other, well… I was willing, to my eternal shame, as Mother says. Frankly, it was just embarrassing, both during and after."

"It?" He pressed for particulars and wanted to kill that unnamed claviger – for his failures, for her disappointment, for touching her at all.

She was brave in her confession. "Not exactly what I expected. What I had hoped."

"You knew to hope for something? How advanced was your education beforehand?" He was surprised, not critical. Americans were a strange lot.

But she took it as censure. "I'm perfectly able to read, Major! It's amazing what you can find in bookstores these days. Boston is a *very* cosmopolitan city. Frankly, now that it's all over, I've no clue what all the fuss is about."

"Now that, my Lazuli, I *can* show you."

Faith wasn't trying to be tempting or coy.

It *had* been mostly embarrassing. That one experience with a man. Oh, Kit had been nice enough. She had genuinely liked him and found him handsome – boyish and dark-haired, with smiling eyes. He was funny, too, an actor and yet amiable, with unaffected address.

But the carnal act itself had been, in a word, disappointing. Clammy and awkward and uncomfortable, and briefly painful, and then with him rutting over her, colored mainly by regret – that she had risked so much for so little.

She could admit none of this to Major Channing, but his eyes in the dark of the small forest gleamed like a true wolf.

Come into the woods, little girl.

I will. I will follow you into darkness.

Faith could not deny the risk was there again, for her to take. Passion and desire, just a taste, or maybe he offered more. It would not matter this time; nothing mattered this time. Regardless of how much he wished from her, wished to take, he could not get her pregnant. He could never give her that.

Faith had thought that, with the act itself being so abysmal, it must only be the results that drove women into conjugal relations. That in being defiled, a woman would at least get something out of it in the long run. Not so for her.

Nevertheless, even swamped by disappointed dreams and broken hopes, still she *hungered*. Faith had been cheated as well as humiliated. And here was a man who could not take her virginity even as she could not take his child. There was an odd kind of freedom to it. And freedom made her bold. She thought she might finally understand what had truly been denied her those many months earlier. When she had yearned and risked and earned nothing but someone else's sweat and a lifetime of regrets.

Faith knew how to catch Channing, too. For she had

taken note of all the times his firm hands had tightened at her back while they danced, and catalogued the many ways his cool eyes moved over her. She had a very good idea of how to be bold with a werewolf. With *this* werewolf.

She tilted her head back and offered him the long, soft column of her throat.

His breath hitched and the ice chips glittered above her, like snowflakes set in alabaster.

He was gentle with her, which she had not expected and wasn't sure she entirely wanted or deserved. His lips were soft and cool and sure. He kissed behind the muscle of her jaw, and along the tendon of her neck, he licked into the divot of her collar bones – his tongue hot and raspy. He grazed the muscle of her shoulder with his teeth but did not bite.

"More," she said. *Too light, too timid, too like the other time.*

His lips, when they pressed over hers, stayed calm and unhurried.

That wasn't what she wanted from him. She wanted the arrogance and the anger. She needed the harshness of winter – overwhelming and unrelenting.

She drew away, examined his face, shadowed and aloof.

"Do you want me to struggle?" she asked. "Am I prey?"

He did not say anything, but his eyes burned hot for long enough to answer her with need. So, she pushed back from him, jerking herself away. She let herself glory in the rush of fighting and fear, of discovery and panic.

Want me enough to keep me, to make me stay.

He jerked her back and slammed his mouth on hers. And it was not kind or gentle; it was harsh and bruising like he must eat into her, devour her with his wanting.

She needed that so very badly – him not to be able to help himself. She wanted the fierceness of unfettered desire.

She whimpered and that seemed to stir him on. His hands were just this side of too strong now, immortal in their ability to hold her tightly to him – forever if he liked.

She pushed up against his unyielding body, bit him back with her small, square teeth. Inferior teeth. She dug her nails into his neck, for at some point she had wrapped her arms up and around him.

It was glorious.

She had searched for this so hard and so far.

She had crossed an ocean for this.

And then it was gone.

And so was he.

After the Brophys' ball, Faith wasn't sure what she expected.

Maybe a declaration.

Maybe a proposal, or more likely, given his character, a proposition. Major Channing might arrange an assignation or set her up as his mistress. She found she did not care for his intent so long as she got to have him. *I have sunk into true depravity.* She shivered in delight.

More likely, what she truly expected was for him to entirely ignore her or to leave town.

She expected anything but indifferent treatment and standoffish regard, which was what she got. She did not see him at any more social events, but she did see him in the hat shop.

He tilted his own hat coolly in her direction.

Faith was not at Chapeau de Poupe to buy anything, and had long since made no pretense at doing so. She came to gossip and to see Biffy while the Iftercasts perused the merchandise.

Faith had her derby on at a jaunty angle, paired with a grey wool split-skirt ensemble, with dozens of tiny brass buttons up the front and decorating the sleeves, and high bicycle boots. She looked well in it; simple, figure-flattering, and elegant by contrast to all the wide-sleeved, elaborate walking dresses around her. She was modern and chic and Biffy approved.

Still, it wasn't enough.

For like all the times before, it seemed that whenever she arrived, Major Channing was just leaving.

"I work, you know," he barked at her when she said, in all desperation, "Must you leave so soon, Major?"

Faith bowed her head to hide the press of tears and raised a hand to touch her neck, which now only faintly showed the places his mouth had once been.

When she looked up, Channing was gone, and Biffy was watching her, eyes full of sympathy and calculation.

"You confuse him greatly." The Alpha was busy folding scarves and arranging them in a fan shape on one of the display cases. Faith was keeping him company, at his request.

"*I* confuse *him*?"

"You will not be shaped into any form with which he is familiar. Immortals, you know, even young ones, are easily overcome by the unexpected. We have a tendency to see the world as predictable. It is rather wondrous to watch Channing struggle."

"It's rather less *wondrous* to be experiencing it from my end."

"I have no doubt of that."

"And yet you yourself seem much more flexible."

Biffy smiled. "I'm very young, for an immortal. Not yet a century." He looked up at a delicate clearing of the throat. "Ah, Mrs Iftercast. You've decided upon that one, have you? Excellent choice. Let me just show you to the counter."

Mrs Iftercast looked worried herself, no doubt having observed Major Channing's precipitous departure. Nevertheless, she smiled brightly and spoke of hats. Faith blessed her for it. Really, she did not know what she would do without the Iftercasts.

Biffy said, as they were leaving, "You are still coming to dine with us, the night after next?" It had been arranged for several weeks now.

Mrs Iftercast nodded adamantly.

Faith knew that, no matter what else occurred, an invitation to dine at Falmouth House was not to be turned down at any cost. So rarely was anyone invited to visit with the London Pack in their own home, it was a social coup. Such *particular* attention to the Iftercasts, once it became widely known, would give rise to rumors of imminent engagements. Everyone had seen the Major's out-of-character focus on the visiting American cousin. And she was *an original*, and very pretty, even if her choice of daytime attire was considered by many too esoteric even for the French. However, werewolves were known to be eccentric in their romantic tastes.

Faith answered for them, because it had to be her decision, as she was the injured party. "We intend to be there and are honored by your thoughtfulness, my lord."

The Alpha reached forward, understanding in his beautiful eyes, and squeezed her hand. "Professor Lyall will be in attendance and eager to renew your acquaintance."

Faith managed a smile. "Good." She had not seen the Beta but the once, at her first ball.

Mrs Iftercast asked, "And will all the rest of the pack be there as well, my lord?"

"Likely most. They are not so very predictable in their activities, I'm afraid. But I expect a full house."

No mention was made of Major Channing by name, but Faith felt warned and warm and worn all at the same time. Biffy was telling her that he would likely be in attendance and that she should brace for battle.

"My dear cousin," Mrs Iftercast pressed, as they steamed back home in the privacy of the family's Isopod, "I shouldn't ask, of course, but his attentions were very marked. And now they are anything but. Was there no formal understanding at all between you? I thought that we had cause to hope. Did you put him off somehow?"

Teddy jumped in, glaring at her mother. "We all know the major is not the type to marry, Mums. Perhaps it is none of Faith's doing."

"Of course, my dear, of course. How thoughtless of me. It's simply that we of the *ton* have never seen him behave so, not towards an unmarried girl. We thought, perhaps, that he was making an exception in your case. That you were somehow different – special."

Foolish of me, thought Faith, *I believed that, too. I believed I understood him – a hundred-year-old supernatural creature. And I blithely made a play for passion. I wouldn't have minded if nothing more materialized beyond that. At least, I think I wouldn't have minded. And he was there, with me. I know he was. He was mine. I made him burn. Except I lost him, and I've no idea why.*

STEP SEVEN

Remember: Either You Are At Dinner or You Are Dinner

Major Channing had taken to coming home very late, or very early in the morning, whichever way you care to look at it, to avoid encountering the rest of his pack. This was not uncommon behavior, especially since the household had accidentally obtained two small children. But he had become more pointed about it.

He had an excuse, as there was a lead in some important BUR business. Those missing Sundowner bullets had, it appeared, been sold to a vampire. So, his professional attentions were now focused on England's hives. This entailed paying formal calls and making very delicate inquiries *himself*, as none of his agents had enough social standing to visit vampires with impunity. So, it had to be Channing, much to his annoyance. He was, to put no small claw on it, uncomfortable around vampires. Unfortunately, nothing more had come of even his best, most polite enquiries, which drove Channing to distraction. It was beyond frustrating that he'd been driven to socialize with *vampires* and still nothing. He'd been polite, for goodness sake. Polite!

Channing was beginning to think that if the blood-suckers had sunk their fangs into his bullets, he might never get them back. He tried to be a little happy that at least the assets were in supernatural hands, and not in those of the Separatists. Nevertheless, he would have liked to have had some assurances one way or the other.

Major Channing hated dealing with vampires – they smelled abominable, were more arrogant than he was, and unconscionably sadistic. It put him in a terrible temper. He had a propensity to bite heads figuratively, because he could not do so literally (not without causing a great fuss, too much paperwork, and no little indigestion). His favorite vampire memories were those abroad, when his old Alpha, Lord Vulkasin, had given him free rein to tear his way through Europe, where hives were ostracized and it was open season on vampires (quite rightly). They tasted awful, vampires did, but Channing still loved to hunt them. As a wolf, he was never happier than with his jaws around the white neck of a blood-sucker, especially a French one. Even as a moon-mad beast, Channing remembered being caged like a dog. For that alone, he would never forgive them, but he had further reason to hate.

Oh, he had learned to bow and scrape and suck up (not like that) with the English vampires, because he must and because they were different from those on the Continent. London vampires dictated high society's rules, so Channing played nice by default. But French vampires? Or Italian? Channing imagined tearing into their necks with such ferocity, he might sever heads from bodies. He imagined it in great detail because he knew the exact particulars of such a maneuver, because he had done it, once, to a vampire queen. The rush of satisfaction had been so all-consuming, it was as close to a sensation of real joy he had felt since he'd been turned into a werewolf.

All this to say that Channing hated vampires. Dealing with them made him even grumpier and more sarcastic than usual. And his feelings of annoyance were certainly *not* exacerbated by a blue-eyed American girl with stones in her heart and honey in her mouth.

God, she tasted sweet. And forbidden. She had yielded with such willingness. As though she knew he needed her surrender almost more than her embrace. He wanted to consume her. Instincts cried out to inhale her – blood sweet and rich, skin soft and warm, the smell of rum and raisins and sugar all around him. She was exactly everything a vampire queen was not, and in that profound difference he might find peace. He'd spent so long wallowing in petty thoughts of revenge – he was all sharp points, harsh and churlish. Sometimes, he wondered what he might become if that did not make up the lion's share of his personality.

Channing had come over all lily-livered, choosing to investigate missing bullets and visit hives (which he loathed) over social engagements (which he had once loathed but now craved).

Not strong enough to entirely resist her presence, Channing slipped into the hat shop on occasion, simply to smell her. Knowing he could control his baser instincts with his Alpha present, but parched for the raisins in her breath and the lapis in her eyes.

Biffy was waiting for Channing as he closed the front door of Falmouth House behind him. Channing snorted at him. It was close to dawn and the Alpha should be in bed with his Beta like any decent Biffy.

"I worried that perhaps you would not make it back in time."

"I always make it back."

His Alpha was sitting in the drawing room, curtains drawn against the rising sun and everything dark around him. He was strong enough to take daylight if he must, even with his youth, but he could not stand it for very long.

Channing could barely withstand a moment of sun and rarely bothered to test himself anymore.

"The Iftercasts are coming to dine here, the night after next."

Channing said nothing in response to this and did not move to join his Alpha in the drawing room.

"Faith will be with them." Biffy answered the question Channing had not asked.

Of course she will. That is why you invited them.

"You will be there, Channing. This is not a request. It is an order from your Alpha. If nothing else, you owe the girl common courtesy, as you have not dignified her with an explanation for your erratic behavior. Your hot-and-cold treatment of her has been shabby in the extreme."

Channing hung his head and still said nothing. There was no excuse. His Alpha was correct.

"Tell her what was done to you, Channing, all those years ago. She has suffered her own version of abuse – she will not be unsympathetic. You need not protect her from it. Then, when you leave her because you are not strong enough to stay and fight to overcome the past, she will at least understand that it was not her fault. You owe her that much. Tell her."

"Or you will?" Channing's tone was bitter.

Biffy stood and walked to him, fine-boned and refined. A dandy. And a werewolf. And an Alpha.

My Alpha.

"You know I would never betray a confidence, even though your history was told to me by others. But I cannot make promises for the rest of the pack."

"Lyall," growled Channing. "You will have Lyall do it."

Biffy straightened, proud and commanding. "It should come from *you*."

Channing left him then, walking slowly through the hallway and up the stairs towards his quarters.

Biffy said to his retreating back, "You will be at this dinner, Gamma."

"I will," whispered Channing, to the shadows of the staircase. Knowing his Alpha would hear him no matter how softly he spoke.

Accordingly, the Iftercasts and their American cousin went to dinner at Falmouth House, in Greenwich.

This was widely remarked upon.

The London Pack did not keep an Isopod steam conveyance, so when one pulled up and disgorged a family of mortals, one of whom was noted to have been courted by a pack member, bets were placed.

A reporter, haunting the street nearby, took note of the elegance of the dinner dresses and number in the party.

Mr Iftercast was in attendance, a clear sign pointing towards marriage negotiation. Miss Wigglesworth looked very fine, if a tad pale, in her gown of peach silk. That fact would appear in the *Mooning Standard* gossip rags the next day as "peach, clearly indicating anticipation and eagerness on the part of the young lady."

Notes were made as to the whiteness of her neck, the trimness of her waist. Notes were not made about the firmness of her jaw and the hardness of her eyes.

Faith thought her dress very daring: the neckline was low and the bodice pleated in such a way as to be extremely flattering. Her pallor was the result of discomfort. She wasn't certain, after a week of so little contact directly following such profound intimacies, how she could calmly sit at table with Major Channing.

The marks on her neck had faded and with them the last of her confidence. Perhaps he did not want her and had never wanted her. Maybe it had all been some kind of game. *Chase me. Chase you.*

Tonight was likely to be an awkward business.

Falmouth House was impressive, appearing more like a very large cottage than a true manor house. It was unexpectedly welcoming and homey, for all its size. It must boast many rooms, considering the entire London pack, its clavigers, and assorted staff all called it home, and yet it felt intimate. It was situated on rising ground outside the village of Blackheath, and with the heath itself nearly surrounding it. It was still *technically* part of London, Mrs Iftercast assured Faith, but rather more towards the outskirts than a lady of high fashion would prefer. Faith supposed wolves needed a place to hunt in their bestial forms (as opposed to the hunting they did in drawing rooms). Faith did not consider herself a lady of high fashion, so she liked both the house and its situation.

Most of the pack members were present to welcome them, including Major Channing. A few were out of town or on business that could not be avoided.

Of those present, Faith had already met Biffy, Professor Lyall, Mr Bluebutton, and Mr Quinn. As to the rest, they were all large, handsome gentlemen of various iterations. Packs apparently did not bother to try to balance the company at table. At Falmouth House, the men vastly outnumbered the women and likely always would.

Faith tried to remember all their names, but found only Mr Hemming and Mr Ditmarsh stuck in her head. Mr Ditmarsh because he was so ridiculously handsome, like the swoon-worthy hero of some Gothic romance, with long dark hair like a pirate and piercing hazel eyes, and Mr Hemming because he was by far the most convivial. He appeared to be something on the order of a country bumpkin, built to till fields and strip his jacket off under the hot sun. His open, friendly countenance resulted in everyone who met him liking him immediately.

The food was simple but very well prepared and prettily presented. There was meat in every dish, and the werewolves ate mainly that and left any vegetables to the guests.

The conversation was stilted at first as the courses were brought out.

"Where, exactly, is your family from, in America,

Miss Wigglesworth?" asked Mr Quinn.

"Boston." Faith hoped they would not ask too much about her family history.

"And do you miss it there?"

"Not especially."

"Stop prying, Quinn," barked Channing, utterly without provocation. "She's here now."

A pause.

Faith glanced up from her food. Biffy's expression was all amusement, Professor Lyall's resignation, and the rest of the pack's nervousness. She did not know what Channing's expression was; she refused to look at him.

Mr Hemming tried next. "And are you enjoying London, Miss Wigglesworth?"

"Yes, more than I thought." Faith smiled at him, grateful for his willingness to face the major's unreasonable ire. *Really, what was Channing about? Just sitting there making everyone else uncomfortable?*

Faith pushed on, doing her part to encourage conversation. "It's such fun here and has been unexpectedly welcoming. Which I'm sure can be attributed to Lord Falmouth's influence and my dear cousins' gracious hospitality."

"How do you find it different from your past society?" Quinn asked.

"Balls are much more frequent here," said Faith.

"Or perhaps here you are simply a great deal more popular," praised Biffy from the head of the table.

Faith could feel her face get hot. "I think it's actually that here there's more opportunity to enjoy oneself."

"Have you plans for when the season has ended?" asked Mr Ditmarsh.

"Oh. No. I hadn't thought that far ahead." *I was supposed to be married or at least engaged. I cannot go home.*

"She'll stay with us, of course," said Teddy, staunchly.

"I cannot possibly continue to trespass on your hospitality. You've been too kind already." Faith said what she ought and trembled with it.

Mrs Iftercast look pointedly at Channing. "Perhaps it will not be a concern."

"I should go home." Faith tried to keep the misery out of her voice.

"We shall see," said Biffy. "I think we could find you a good match. One of my boys, perhaps."

The gentlemen arranged about the table all looked highly uncomfortable, but none of them would contradict their Alpha. A few side-eyed their Gamma with trepidation.

Biffy looked mischievous. He gestured at Mr Bluebutton. "Adelphus here is, of course, quite elegant and cultivated. One might think him respectable, but he has the reputation of a philanderer, so perhaps not."

The werewolf in question rolled his eyes. "No worse than Channing, and we all know—" He stopped abruptly, as if someone had kicked him under the table.

Biffy moved on to his next victim.

"Quinn is an utter sweetheart, and punctilious by nature, but his temper occasionally gets the better of him, particularly around vampires."

"I say!" said Quinn. "Me? Channing is ten times worse if blood-suckers are—" Another abrupt cut-off.

Faith was beginning to be entertained by the show. Biffy was trying to amuse her at the expense of his long-suffering pack. It was rather sweet of him.

On his host's left, Mr Iftercast gave concerted attention to his meal in a desperate manner that suggested he had absolutely no idea what to do under these particular circumstances. Teddy and her brothers were all wide-eyed and interested in this teasing game, maybe seeing some of their own sibling rivalries amongst the werewolves. Mrs Iftercast looked partly amused, partly horrified.

Biffy continued with a nod at Mr Ditmarsh, who stopped eating, crossed his arms, and stared at his Alpha – as if daring him to do his damnedest.

Biffy said, "Ulric here might be a little too old for you, Faith dear, and a *great* deal too autocratic. Although perhaps you could bring him down a peg or two?"

Faith giggled.

Ulric said, clearly entering into the spirit of the thing, "I'd be delighted to give her the opportunity to find out. I enjoy a challenge."

Channing grumbled, "Enjoy a challenge, do you? Outside, right now, wolf form, try me."

Mr Ditmarsh hid a smile and tilted his head to show his neck to the Gamma. He clearly knew his rank. He was also clearly delighted to see Channing getting more and more annoyed, as each subsequent pack member was offered up as a candidate for Faith's affections.

Faith was beginning to enjoy it, too, as it became clear the only werewolf truly made uncomfortable at the table was Major Channing. Although it was slightly at her expense. Still, the idea of a werewolf buffet, all because she had a reputation as a tail-chaser, was a fair cop.

She was *not enjoying* Channing's reactions, because she was determined not to let anything that impossible man did affect her anymore. But the gentle banter between the Alpha and his pack was adorable. Very family-like and comforting.

She tried for pert and innocent. "And what about Mr Hemming? What flaws could he possibly have?"

Hemming blushed, which Faith didn't think werewolves could do. It was boyish and amiable.

Biffy chuckled. "Oh, you like Hemming, do you?"

Channing growled, actually growled, at the dinner table.

Now it was Faith's turn to blush.

"No concerns there, my dear, everyone likes Hemming. He's easy to like, aren't you, Ian?"

Hemming grinned, pleased by the praise and the affection in his Alpha's voice. "So, Alpha, what's wrong with me, then? Won't I make a good husband for this charming young lady?"

"Of course you will, dear, you're quite lovely."

Faith glanced down at the Beta at the other end of the table, only to find Professor Lyall eating quietly with a small, indulgent smile on his face. Clearly, he was entirely unthreatened by his Alpha's obvious affection for the rest of their pack.

Is that what it's like to be loved by a werewolf? So confident in his adoration and fidelity that you can watch him tease others without rancor? Or is that a Beta trait? Not for the first time, Faith wished she knew more about werewolf pack dynamics and courting rituals.

"But Hemming is very occupied with the children at present." Biffy formulated a well-crafted excuse. "He has no time for romance."

Mrs Iftercast jumped desperately on that opening. "Oh, yes, you have two infants in residence, I've been given to understand. Do please tell us about the dear little things?"

Biffy was willing to temporarily give over his game of Torment Channing in the interest of common courtesy. "My pleasure. Gracie came along with the nanny we hired for Robbie, our foundling. So, we find ourselves looking after two of the darlings. Or Mrs Whybrew does. Powerful presence, Mrs Whybrew, but a very good nanny. Robbie's recently started talking. And Gracie crawls everywhere and gets into everything."

"Are you fond of children, my lord?"

"Fond enough, fond enough. It helps when they are not one's own, I feel. Not that Robin isn't considered part of this pack, but it's mostly Quinn and Hemming who take an active interest in his upbringing."

Mrs Iftercast took that as an opportunity to probe. "Not Major Channing?" She turned to glance pointedly at Channing, who was obviously in a fine temper and as a result ought to be ignored. She quickly returned her attention to Biffy.

"Channing's relationship with children is... complex."

Mr Bluebutton, looking crafty, undid all of Mrs Iftercast's good work. "So, what about Channing then, Alpha, for our Miss Wigglesworth here? Would he not do in a pinch?"

Biffy gave him a gleaming look of approval. "Oh, I don't know, what do you think?"

Comments instantly erupted from all of the werewolves now that permission had been given.

"He's near as bad a flirt as I am, although his preferences are more confined." Mr Bluebutton was clearly referring to having been accused of philandering.

Channing said, "You forget yourself, Adelphus, that was decades ago."

"Oh, of course, you've been a positive monk since when? Eighteen-seventy or so, when Lady Maccon came to the pack and you insulted her to her face." Adelphus sneered at him. "Self-flagellation, perhaps?"

"And don't even get him started on vampires. He's *much* worse than I am," added Quinn.

"To be fair, he has a greater right to be," said one of the other werewolves, Faith thought his name was Zev or Zeb or something odd like that, coming to his Gamma's defence.

"Good point," conceded Quinn.

Faith was wildly curious. *What exactly had the vampires done to Channing that justified such ire?*

Canning stopped eating, crossed his arms, and glared about the table. "Would anyone else like to assassinate my character at dinner?"

"Ooo, me!" said Hemming.

"Yes, Hemming, why am I unsuitable?"

"Well, you don't like children at all, simply because, you know, *that* happened."

One of the others said, "Which is why he doesn't want to marry, either. You know, because of *her*."

Murmurs of agreement.

Her, thought Faith, *her who?* She glared at Biffy, suddenly annoyed by the whole thing. *What on earth is going on here? What are you trying to tell me?*

Biffy was looking pleased with this outcome.

Faith began to get a little angry about the whole thing. It seemed almost cruel to expose Channing thus, even as he had been unkind to her and neglectful. His private feelings and reasons, his past hurts, should stay that way, private and in the past.

She said, staunchly, "Well, thanks, for my part, gentlemen. Your Alpha continually effacing you all as not good enough flatters me greatly. Although it obviously doesn't flatter any of you." The table chuckled.

Faith gave a thought to throwing Teddy to the wolves, diverting attention that way. Encouraging them to offer themselves to her friend in a similarly ridiculous manner. But Teddy's engagement to Mr Rafterwit (and his stables) was now widely known (it had appeared in the papers yesterday); no doubt the werewolves were honoring that commitment by not flirting with her.

(Mr Rafterwit had taken knee to hay bale when he made his offer. He'd been showing her about his stables at the time. Teddy said it was the most romantic thing *ever* and that she was *incandescent* with happiness. Mr Rafterwit promised her the next filly out of his favored stallion for her very own, and swore they would spend at least half the year in the countryside. Teddy was in ecstasies.)

Biffy said, "Surely, one of you might do?" As though he were some matchmaking mamma and it hardly mattered which. "I hadn't even finished the table, Miss Wigglesworth. Don't you find any of my pack handsome enough to suit?"

"Very. All of them."

Biffy nodded. "And, of course, there is also Rafe, who is away and very appealing if you like the rough and ready. And Riehard. Well, Riehard could be anything you wanted him to be."

What if I want him tall and blond and moody, with icy eyes and a sour disposition? What if I want him to throw me up against the wall and press against me with his whole body, as if he needed me to breathe? Would he send me rocks and take me to geology meetings? Would he learn my history and not care that some other man had taken me first?

"Enough!" said Channing, at last.

Biffy sat back, expression smug.

Faith hid a smile.

In classic wolf fashion, Channing's Alpha sat at the head of the table. His Beta, however, sat opposite, at the foot, a position ordinarily occupied by the lady of the house.

Channing preferred this arrangement; it meant Lyall and Biffy couldn't bill and coo and share private secrets during meals. They still made eyes at one another, engaging in that silent form of communication which all couples develop over time and reminds those who are not entangled of what they are missing. Channing thought such displays of affection were vulgar, emotional wealth worn wreathed about a man like too many strands of pearls.

Channing looked at Faith, wondering if he could do that with her, right now. Silently communicate. And what would he say if he could?

But she was not looking at him.

Which of course made him burn with the need for her immediate attention.

His Alpha had warned him. He had known he would be in for it at this gathering. So, here they all sat, the pack backing Biffy, worrying at Channing as if he were a juicy bone to pick at.

It had worked. Of course it had worked. He'd lost his temper and barked at them all.

Fortunately, the bickering and pseudo match-making had carried them through the entirety of dinner. They adjourned to the drawing room for wine and light petits fours instead of a pudding course.

Channing watched Faith's lithe figure as she was led through by Professor Lyall. He thought her dress was very daring and impossibly flattering. There was nothing to distract or detract from the delicacy of her bone structure or the trimness of her waist. The gown's neckline was low, the decoration a simple cream ribbon.

He wanted to rip it off her.

Naturally, the pack arranged it so he was seated next to her.

At that juncture, the pack put in a concerted effort to distract the Iftercasts and give Channing and Faith some measure of privacy. Adelphus and Biffy held Mrs Iftercast and Teddy's attention with gossip of the *ton*, making up outrageous stories about who was engaged to whom and whether it was a love match or merely a polite arrangement. Lyall and Quinn talked matters of politics and business with Mr Iftercast in serious tones. Ulric and Hemming chatted amiably with the Iftercasts' male children on inconsequential matters over cards. There was much laughter among them.

Zev and Phelan, the most reserved of the pack, made their excuses and went about their evening's business. Channing wished he could do the same, but he was under orders to remain.

So, he sat in one corner, out of human hearing, with Miss Wigglesworth. To whom he had indeed been rather shabby.

He owed her an explanation or at least an apology.

However, because she was staunch and forthright and oh so darling, Faith took the opening afforded by their comparative isolation before he could. Brave, his Lazuli. Shining with courage, not afraid of anything, not even him.

"You've reconsidered my history and decided against me, sir?"

Is that what she thinks? I have made her doubt herself further.

"Never that." He resisted pressing her hand.

"You're afraid I'd insist on matrimony? I promise, I wouldn't." Faith lowered her voice to almost a whisper. "I'd take you however I could get you."

That jolted him with need. He noticed his marks on her neck had faded, and he hated that. He wanted her under him and writhing, trying to escape, helpless. His in every way. The scent of her filling him, the body of her being filled.

"You have no idea what you offer."

"You forget, sir. I know *exactly* what I offer."

"You should be demanding I marry you. Your family should have me horsewhipped for what I did to you in that garden. There should be a gun with silver bullets to my head and you waiting for me at the altar."

"Is that what you want?" She was clearly confused.

He took a breath. "Whichever way I took you – one night, one season, or all of your eternity – I would be no good for you. I want you. God's teeth, of course I want you. *Look* at you. You are perfect."

She leaned in, eyes bright. "Is it your nature that makes you give up before we've even started? I promise,

I'd run from you every night. Chase me. Mark me."

Channing felt himself tighten full-body, swollen and straining with want. He feared the others might smell his arousal. *I am no good for you.* He couldn't speak.

"You gave me rocks. You took me to a scientific lecture. You make me *need* so much. It isn't fair to let me drift like this. Where will I anchor if not to you?"

"I warned you I was a cad."

"You don't think you're good enough for me?"

"I don't think I can change enough to suit you."

"Then let me go. Cut me loose. Truly stop this."

But you are mine. His heart beat the refrain – *mine mine mine* – pushing old dead blood through tired immortal veins. He was exhausted and lonely.

"I am trying to," he said.

"Try harder," she snapped back.

Channing did not realize until later that night how alike they were. How, this time, he had thrown down the gauntlet to her. The island of his loneliness was temptation, summoning Faith to swim towards it. For she had been treading water a long time and saw him as a place of refuge, unexplored. Faith knew he was no safe tropical island, rich with greenery and wholesome fruit. She knew Channing's soul was a granite boulder standing stiff and solitary in the midst of an abandoned lake.

But she would take that as a challenge, his Lazuli. Granite, to her, was full of many fascinating things – minerals and crystals and shards of trapped light. A rock was never only a rock to a geologist.

She had told him to let her go and to run. But she was really saying, *I will track you. I will hunt you. I will follow. And you will smooth the water with your own ice*

STEP EIGHT

Never, Under Any Circumstances, Make a Public Scene

Like a good girl, Teddy waited to turn into a jittering wreck on the way home, thank heavens. Her first comment explained why she'd been so quiet throughout the evening. "Oh, those werewolves, so blunt with their implications. Around the dinner table, no less. I declare, I hardly knew where to look or what to say."

Faith hid a smile and imitated Teddy's accent. "To be sure, cousin, even breathing seemed a risk at times."

"Now you're teasing me, Faith darling. But be serious, we are like sisters now. Do you really want such a thing as that? I mean to say, should you marry Major—"

"Now, Theodora, don't tempt fate," interjected Mrs Iftercast.

Teddy corrected herself. "Should you marry into the London Pack, then, well, that would be your life. Every night sitting around that table with those big loud men." She shuddered. "Hardly bears contemplating."

Faith thought it sounded wonderful.

Colin said to his sister, "Teds, don't be a ninnyhammer. I'm sure Faith feels the same about your prospective future spent mucking about with horses and mulch and oats and sheds and bally whatnot."

Faith nodded vigorously.

Colin gestured. "See there? Mother, now that you've got the girls sorted, could we get on to me and Miss Fernhough? She's such a marvelous pip. I tell you. The pippiest."

Teddy took Faith's hand while the rest of the family attempted to convince Colin that no matter how pippy his Miss Fernhough, she was still too young.

"Of course, Faith dear, if you like him, then I am with you 'til the bitter end."

"Well, I hope it doesn't come to that, but thanks, Teddy."

Accordingly, Faith became even more determined in her pursuit of one arrogant blond werewolf. The pack was on her side. The Iftercasts were on her side. Surely even Major Channing could not stand against all of them?

Faith decide to seriously strategize. She began to research. She made enquiries. She learned all she could about werewolves in general and the enigmatic Major Channing in particular. His war record was extensive. His reputation was colorful. His previous relationships were temporary. His history before he became a werewolf was… absent. Oh, there were rumors: that he'd been a sculptor and then a soldier, and that he'd been bitten in battle during one of Napoleon's many wars.

She learned that his current place of business, BUR headquarters, was located in Fleet Street. She sourced his other haunts. His club was Claret's. He preferred to walk and to run on Blackheath and not in Hyde Park. His contacts and compatriots were primarily within the War Office, the Home Office, and the military barracks.

She found a painting of a white wolf bent and drinking at the edge of a half-frozen lake, the world white around him. The artist was skilled, breezy in his brush strokes so that the very stillness of the image hinted at a burst of motion soon to come, the moment that the wolf looked up and noticed he was observed.

It cost more than she could afford and less than it was worth, but she bought it anyway and sent it 'round to Falmouth House, directed to Major Channing.

He had sent her courting gifts. Hunted rocks and laid them at her feet like fresh kill. She would do the same.

She found a pair of slippers made of rabbit fur and, highly amused at her own daring, ordered a size she hoped would fit, and sent those next. Directed to Major Channing, with no inscription, and no return address.

She thought it likely that he'd find such trinkets very annoying, and that the others would laugh at his expense. But then, late at night, he might put on the slippers and look at the painting and think of her.

Her campaign was probably going as well as she could hope. She hadn't seen Channing in several days, but Biffy positively beamed at her when she dropped by the hat shop.

"What are you up to, little American?" he teased. "Our boy is flustered. I've never seen him flustered before."

"Killing him with kindness," said Faith.

"That's no joke. With Channing, it might actually kill him."

So, she was feeling almost optimistic.

Until her parents came to town.

It was Teddy who told her.

"Oh, Faith, you'll never believe it, but your mother and father have just arrived in town. They are downstairs in the hallway."

Faith felt sick. "What?"

"Apparently, Mums wrote them. Ages ago, right after we visited the hat shop the first time. Mums was so chuffed, you see? After such noted attention from Lord Falmouth, she felt certain we would be announcing your engagement imminently. And to a werewolf, no less, exactly as your parents wanted. Then, when Major Channing began to avoid you, she forgot to write again to warn them off. It likely wouldn't have done any good. They had already set out across the Atlantic. They came by *steamer*, if you would believe it? Not by dirigible. In this day and age, so old-fashioned. No offense."

"Well, they *are* old-fashioned, but really, Mother hates floating." Faith was still in shock. *There're here. Why are they here? Mother hates London. It's full of monsters.*

"Oh, heavens!" Faith collapsed back onto her bed. "Do they expect to stay here, too? Is there room for them? And if not, will I have to go with them to a hotel?"

"Why, Faith, you're trembling. Of course you must remain with us regardless. You *will* stay here with us! You're proper family."

"But... appearances."

"Hang appearances! I'm sure Mums will make the

offer, but it would be very cramped quarters if they accepted. You're already in Charlie's room, so Cyril and Colin would have to double up. They hate doing that."

"My parents can afford to stay somewhere else." Faith was upset on her host's behalf. "Trust me, Teddy dear, you don't want them here."

Teddy nodded, glumly. "I told Mums they were perfectly *horrid* to you. I thought Mums understood what that meant. But you know how absentminded she gets. And she never takes me seriously. She'll invite them to stay. We can only pray your parents understand the limits of this household and decline on the basis of convenience."

"Agreed," said Faith.

Teddy eyed the door. "Should we go down, do you think?"

"I suppose it would look strange if I didn't. They're *my* parents, after all. Save yourself, Teddy, and stay up here."

"I should never let you go into battle alone!" Teddy was fierce.

Faith pressed her cousin's hand. "You are a dear and loyal friend."

So it was that Faith and Teddy marched down the grand staircase together. Faith clutched Teddy's burly little arm for support. Teddy wore a militant look upon her round face. Faith looked calm and collected, only the dampness of her grip betraying her weakness.

It's silly, really. It's not as if I didn't live with them for twenty-four years. But for the last few months, in London, Faith had felt both free and safe. It was the best she had ever felt. The Iftercasts had given her a home for the very first time in her life, a true sanctuary. Now, knowing it was possible to find family a comforting environment, the very idea of returning to the withered bosom of her former life seemed not only unfair but cruel.

Fortunately, Faith's parents still did not want her. But they did want to see what she was up to.

They had taken rooms in the Beaumont Hotel, and there was no space for Faith there.

"We hope you don't consider us officious, imposing our wayward daughter upon you a little longer? Only until this engagement, at which you hinted, comes to fruition."

Mrs Iftercast blanched and looked desperately at Faith. Faith shook her head slightly. *By all means, let my parents think I have the protection of a pack along with a prospective husband.*

"Speaking of which, Faith, where's your maid?"

It was such an entirely unexpected inquiry, and such sudden focused attention from her mother, that Faith started. "Minnie?"

"Why, do you suddenly have some *other* maid?"

"She's not here."

"Not here. What do mean, *not here*? Have you misplaced her? Are you going around London randomly scattering maids to the four corners?"

"No. She's on loan to my seamstress."

"What?" Mrs Wigglesworth went positively purple about the face. "Why on earth?"

"Minnie is handy with her needle, and my need for dresses outweighed my need for her assistance at home."

"Well, that explains the appalling state of your hair."

Faith touched her coiffure, a perfectly innocuous twist pinned to her crown with a few curls arranged down one side. Nothing offensive or particularly special about it.

Mrs Wigglesworth persisted. "Where is this wayward maid, exactly? Give me the address of your modiste. I'll go retrieve her immediately."

Faith blinked, surprised. Never had her mother taken much interest in Minnie. A daughter's maid, once safely situated, was beneath Mrs Wigglesworth's notice. They were not at odds, not even after Faith's disgrace. Minnie had never been blamed. Faith supposed, if she thought on it at all, she would have said her mother utterly indifferent to Minnie's very existence. Why the attention now?

Before Faith could protest or make excuses or anything else in an effort to protect poor Minnie, Mrs Iftercast, in a desperate move at mollification, gave Faith's mother Mrs Honeybun's address.

Faith could only hope Minnie was able to hold out.

Faith had, truth be told, been anticipating a conversation regarding termination of services. Minnie seemed far better suited to Mrs Honeybun's employ. The shop had grown popular amongst the more daring set of sporting young ladies. After *the original* Miss Wigglesworth, favored intimate of Lord Falmouth, was known to acquire all her dresses there, the orders fairly floated in.

Minnie loved it. Faith was happy to see her so pleasantly situated. There were far more opportunities for a girl in such a skilled position than there were as a lady's maid. It would be nice if one of them got what they wanted out of London.

Mrs Wigglesworth, address in hand and apparently satisfied, returned her attention to the matter of Faith's position. "So, this engagement?"

Mrs Iftercast said in an effort at diversion, "There is a reception of some note at the National Gallery this evening. Would you like to attend? Many of London's celebrated supernatural luminaries will be there. You know, vampires and werewolves. Art events are considered neutral ground."

Mrs Wigglesworth pursed her lips. "Sounds awful."

Mrs Iftercast blanched. "Oh, but if you wish to see Faith's..."

"I suppose, if we must."

"You go," said Mr Wigglesworth. "I've business to conduct while we're here."

His wife looked even more sour than usual at being thrown to the wolves. "Oh, but—"

Faith braced herself, prepared for her mother's temper to make an appearance.

"Very *important* business, my dear. Remember?" Only that tone in her father's voice could quell her mother's wrath. Faith winced. What were her parents up to?

She simpered. "Oh, yes, Hubert dear. I remember."

Accordingly, it was with a heavy heart for all concerned, even the Iftercasts, who were beginning to understand how lucky they were to have received Faith (and not one of the other Wigglesworths) into their happy home, that they set out for the gallery that evening. The party was composed of Mrs Iftercast and her daughter accompanying Mrs Wigglesworth and her daughter. The gentlemen, to a man, had bowed out.

Channing had no good reason for being at the National Gallery that night, but he was grateful for it, in the end. He was not surprised when Faith entered the gathering along with the Iftercast ladies. If anything, he was delighted, although he did not let that show in word or deed.

There was one other female with them – an older, sour-faced rabbity woman with beady eyes. Much to his shock, instead of playing any kind of game, Faith led this new female directly towards him.

Ulric was standing next to him. "Who's that with our little Faith?" He was already sounding protective. As if she were pack.

"Another American," snorted Channing.

"How do you know? Have you met her before?"

"No, but would you look at her? Americans always gesture the biggest and walk the slowest."

"Our little Faith is not like that."

"Stop calling her that."

"You would prefer I said *your* little Faith?"

"Hush, Ulric, they're approaching."

Faith had desperate eyes.

Channing instantly wanted to do anything to make that look go away. He made a small bow to her and the strange female, as did Ulric.

"Gentlemen, allow me to make my mother known to you? Mother, this is Major Channing and Mr Ditmarsh, of the London *Werewolf* Pack."

The female gave them both a highly offensive once-over. Her narrowed eyes seemed to judge them lower than dirt.

My lovely, bright girl came from this creature?

"You're a werewolf?" Her voice could strip

wallpaper.

Channing was too old to bandy insults, but he did enjoy it so. "You are a human female?"

The lady bristled. "I bleed red, sir!"

"It was not the *human* part I questioned."

The woman did an interpretive fish expression before going red about the ears and whirling to her daughter. Her voice was now cold and vicious. "He's not what I expected, daughter. Not at all what I wanted. I don't know about this."

Channing went to say something even worse, to bring her attention and anger back to him and shield Faith, but Ulric beat him to it.

Ulric might enjoy abusing Channing as much as possible amongst pack-mates, but he would never stand idly by and permit anyone *non-pack* to abuse him. Ulric glared at the repugnant female. "Major Channing is a decorated soldier, the head of a powerful government body, reasonably tall, and passably good-looking. He has all his teeth, all his hair, and all his limbs. What more could you possibly wish for in a son-in-law?"

"Oh, but Mr Dickswamp—"

"Ditmarsh."

"Mr Dickmark. I meant no offense to your – how do you say it? – pack-bud."

"Pack-*mate*," Ulric gritted out through clenched teeth.

"Whatever. I meant to say that I expected something *less*. Even with that attitude, he is probably too good for my worthless daughter." Faith's mother whirled back to face Channing, looking up at him, her face contorted with disgust. He was not sure if that was for him or Faith.

"You don't know my daughter very well, do you, sir, to be actually interested in marrying her?"

Nothing upset Channing more than a mother abusing her own child. This woman was beyond repulsive. They were in public! To say such a thing about her daughter when others could overhear? *Is her intent to humiliate me or Faith or both?* "I know her as well as can be expected, given the restrictions of polite society." He would not defame Faith's character, no matter what had been done to her in the past.

"He's a good man, Mother. Please don't make a scene. Please, your temper."

Mrs Wigglesworth wrinkled her lip. "He is not a *man* at all. I'm shocked you caught him, girl. I didn't think you had it in you."

Channing blinked a moment. *She sent Faith here believing she would fail? Why?*

Faith was looking ever more desperate. As though she was trying to hold her mother back, hold her silent through sheer force of will. Channing hurt with the need to fix this. But he did not know how. Mrs Wigglesworth would not shut up, and she was Faith's *mother*, after all.

People were listening in now. Mrs Wigglesworth's voice was strident and nasal, carrying throughout the gallery. Channing had grown accustomed to Faith's accent, but Faith's voice was calm and smooth, nothing like that of this woman.

He looked down his nose at the female in front of him. She didn't smell right, either, drenched in perfume – chemical flowers and some dead animal's musk. That kind of thing was banned at parties in London. This whole situation was, well, appalling. Channing should know; he had done a number of appalling things in his day.

"My daughter won't make you a good wife, sir."

She continues to sabotage her own daughter? What is going on here?

His Lazuli looked down at her feet and whispered. "But, Mother, I thought you *wanted* me to marry a werewolf." Clearly, she was confused, too.

Channing growled at Mrs Wigglesworth. "She is perfect. Do hush yourself, woman. No one here cares for your good opinion."

"You're making a mistake," warned the lady. Although Channing hesitated to use the word *lady*. *Creature* suited her better. Or was that an insult to other creatures?

Faith obviously did not know what to do. Admit to an attachment, which her mother had once wanted, and prove she had succeeded as instructed, yet be totally undermined? Or admit to no attachment, which her mother now wanted, and be told off for failure? Mrs Wigglesworth had put her daughter in an untenable position. No matter what Faith said, her mother would have an excuse to attack. Which Channing suspected was the woman's real objective.

Finally, Faith admitted, to her slippers, "We are not engaged."

"Well, fine, he's safe from you and your corruption, isn't he? Good thing I arrived in time to warn him, isn't it? Did he have his way with you, too? Did you let him, you whore?"

"Mother!" Faith's voice was cracked and quiet.

"She is broken, Major Channing. If your intent is honorable and decent, you should know that she is neither."

Faith had begun to cry now. Silent tears rolling down out of those blue eyes. Her fists were clenched as well.

The tears were humiliation; the fists were fury.

Channing felt sick. This, then, was Mrs Wigglesworth's objective. To humiliate her daughter on two continents. Revenge for some perceived slight to family name or her own petty vanity. Channing would not have it!

Mrs Iftercast made herself known at this juncture. She put an arm about Faith's waist. "I thought you came to see her settled, cousin. To give your blessing. We all thought you had come to London so the correct forms could be observed." Mrs Iftercast's voice was trembling. Her round face and cubby form fairly vibrated with offence.

Channing said, wishing it was his arm offering comfort, "I begin to think this female crossed the Atlantic merely to shame her daughter in my eyes."

He leaned forward so his mouth almost touched Mrs Wigglesworth's ear. He wrapped one large hand about her upper arm, holding her in place.

"Don't touch me," she spat, "you beast!"

He spoke so quietly, only she could hear him. Well, maybe Ulric could, too, with his supernatural senses, but he was pack, so that was fine. Although with all the murmuring and shocked exclamations at the public scene, his words were masked.

"Madam, you are the mother of the woman I love, and all the things you think I do not know about her, I know. This act of sabotage of yours is petty and foolish, for it will no more dissuade me from anything I chose to do than your piss could divert a river."

She gasped at his crassness and struggled against his grip.

"*Stay still*, or you will see what kind of monster I am."

She froze.

He continued to hiss in her ear. "Faith is ours now. You will leave this country and never return. You will not speak to her. You will not write to her. You will not even look at her again. You think what you have done here, now, ruins her in the eyes of London society? *We* control society." He tilted his head towards Ulric's imposing form, hovering protectively near Faith. "I will drag your name through the gutter as a liar and a mad zealot who comes to destroy her own daughter's relationship out of hatred for the supernatural. Do you think they will side with *an American* over *me*? Over *us*?" He flicked the fingers of his free hand once more towards Ulric, who was at his most gorgeous and pompous. "*We* are the *London Pack. You* are *nothing*. And if you think we will try to preserve your reputation because it is tied to Miss Wigglesworth's, well, then even as I dirty your name, you can be certain I will change hers. I will give her *mine*. And I am one of the Chesterfield Channings."

He let Mrs Wigglesworth go and stepped back.

"Faith," he said, turning to the trembling girl.

She was not afraid; she was humiliated and furious. She was holding it all in, though, and looked only sad. He applauded her for this. Because while he knew her true feelings, others saw only her pretty face, her apparent fragility, and an unwarranted attack.

"Faith, come to me now," he commanded.

She would not look at him, her head resting on Mrs Iftercast's shoulder. Her little round cousin stood at her other side, patting her back and glaring.

"Lazuli."

She raised watery blue eyes to him.

He held out a hand.

She took a step across the divide that separated them within a circle of gawking onlookers. She brushed past her frozen, vibrating harridan of a mother.

He tugged her to him, against his chest, in front of all the assembled.

She gave a little sigh and relaxed infinitesimally. Her smell, sweet cake and candied fruit and intoxicating spirits, flooded his senses.

Ulrich stepped after her, bracketing and shielding her figure with his bulk, hiding her vulnerability from the eyes of others. His brother warrior, protecting his love's unprotected back. As it should be.

Channing said, "Mrs Iftercast, take your cousin away from here."

Mrs Iftercast nodded, still disgusted with Mrs Wigglesworth, but they had all come in the Isopod together. They must leave that way.

Mrs Iftercast was made of solid stock. "Come with me, Mrs Wigglesworth, and I will return you to your hotel. Theodora, stay with Faith. You, sir, Major Channing, I expect a formal announcement in the *Times* for tomorrow."

Channing grinned. He had thought Mrs Iftercast quite silly, but there was iron in her.

"Of course." He nodded, arrogant and regal. *She is mine now.* Curious that his reluctance to remarry was so easily put aside when his Faith needed him. Needed rescuing from her own family. He had realized it must be bad. Not only her childhood growing up amongst such people, but the way they treated her after she fell from grace. The apparently unpardonable sin of exploring her own passion.

Even if I fail her in marriage as I failed my first wife. Even if I am not strong enough for this. She will have the pack. She will have my pack. I can give her that. They will take care of her if I cannot. He looked at Ulric; his pack-mate's face, so impossibly handsome, was furrowed in concern even as he scanned the crowd. On guard for further attack.

But the crowd was with them. They either did not care or, more likely, did not believe the strange older American woman who had hurled abuses at Miss Wigglesworth.

Miss Wigglesworth was the toast of the town. London had adopted her. She was *their* American! How dare another American threaten her? She had taken it upon herself to tame one of the most untamed werewolves in all the *ton*. It wasn't as if Channing had ever been considered eligible. She was welcome to him, no one else wanted him, and they were happy to have her. A Channing tamed by an American was better than an untamed Channing.

Besides, while it made for an embarrassing scene to witness, it was also particularly juicy gossip. Not the least of which being that everyone who was present at the National Gallery that evening knew now that the one werewolf who'd sworn never to marry (well, never to marry a second time, for those whose memories were long enough) was actually *engaged*.

Faith had never suffered through anything more mortifying in her life. After Kit and the discovery of the full repercussions of her indiscretion, things had been *very, very* mortifying. Her mother had been privately cruel, her temper had flared even more than was normal, but she had never publicly shamed Faith before. Faith supposed that in Boston, her mother cared, while in London she did not.

Then to have Mrs Iftercast and Teddy come to her defence, and Channing come to her rescue. Now to find herself engaged! Why, it was as if successive waves of different emotions crashed over her, buffeting her, until all she felt was saturated, shipwrecked, and gasping.

She awoke from the deluge to find herself still curled against her werewolf. His arm, strong and sure, was around her. His scent, wild and masculine, was all she could smell.

"Ulric," said Channing, "clear us a path. Let's get our girl out of here."

Faith found herself moved carefully through a hushed crowd, out of the gallery, and through other showrooms until they were in some small forgotten part of the museum.

"Shut the door, Miss Iftercast."

"But, sir!"

"A moment alone with my betrothed is all I ask. It will not be long enough for me to ravish her, I promise."

The door closed.

Faith said, with confidence learned from her own mistake, "It doesn't take all *that* long."

Channing snorted. "It does if you do it properly." Cool fingers pressed her chin up. "Lazuli, look at me."

"My eyes are all red."

"Your eyes are beautiful and you know it. Here, blow." He pulled out a handkerchief, and Faith made it soggy and tried to repair herself a little.

"So, you won," he said.

"This isn't exactly how I wanted it to go." Faith trembled. They had had such a game going between them, and now it was all over and she had trapped him into marriage, because he had a kind heart and he pitied her.

She took a deep, shaky breath. "I owe you an explanation, Major."

"I think you may call me Channing now that we are engaged."

She was arrested. "What's your first name?"

"That is."

"I don't understand."

"Channing is both my first and last name, because my parents thought they were being particularly cheeky or because they were idiots. I don't know, I never asked them. They died in an experimental yeast fermentation accident when I was three."

She blinked. "There's so much I don't know about you. And there's so much you don't know about me. I should tell you. I must tell you, now, before this engagement is made public."

He quirked an eyebrow.

"Fine, before it's made any *more* public."

"I know the worst of your sins, my Lazuli."

"No." She marshaled her courage. "You don't. That wasn't the whole of it. Otherwise, I would have contradicted Kit's boasting. I could've lied. Werewolves have so little standing in Boston, and Kit was only a claviger. He could've said I flipped my skirts for him, and I could've denied it, truth or not."

"That is not your style." He had such confidence in

her.

"No, it's not. But you've seen my mother. She would've hidden me away, kept me trapped in my room, stopped me from saying anything, and denied it all publicly. In fact, that's exactly what she tried to do. But it wasn't possible, you understand?"

He stopped breathing and drew away from her.

Faith's skin went all over tight and tingled with fear. But she would do this. She owed him honesty. She owed him all her truths. He might keep his own past hidden from her, but she would not be so reticent. If they were to have anything together, it must be based on honesty.

"What happened?" She knew that he did not want the truth, but he asked because she needed him to. Faith loved him for that.

"There was a child." She flopped her hands open in a helpless gesture. "It only takes one time, did you know that? Well, I didn't. But apparently, only once." She gave a humorless little laugh. "Lucky me."

He closed his eyes, clearly horrified. "What happened to the baby, Faith?"

He is no longer calling me Lazuli. She swallowed, her throat parched.

He grabbed her shoulders, pressed her back so she must lean into his hard hands or fall. His gaze was impossibly cold and fierce.

"What did you do to it?"

Faith understood, then, some small part of his past. Not all, of course; he would have to tell her the rest. But she understood the signs of betrayal in others; she had felt it so often herself. "Channing, I'm not her. You know that, don't you?"

"What. Happened. To. The. Baby." A small shake

each time.

"I lost it. Late in the pregnancy. Too late, they tell me. I wonder sometimes if the baby knew, somehow, that it wasn't wanted. So, it rid itself of me." She looked away, closed her own eyes. "There was a lot of blood. They wouldn't even tell me if it was a boy or a girl." She hated describing it. She wanted to shove the memory back where it belonged, locked away as if in the smallest corner of the bottom drawer of her specimen case. A deadly little treasure, like a chunk of cinnabar, that she knew was there, that she had collected, but that would destroy her if she took it out and handled it, dwelt upon it.

He made the funniest sound then, a lost whine-whimpering, and drew her back against him. Arms gentle. But she didn't deserve comfort, so she pushed away, forced herself to go on. *I've got to get this all out now, or I won't have the guts to do it later.*

"No," she said, "Let me finish."

"No more," he begged.

She overruled him. "It damaged me. *The baby* damaged me, tore me open. Inside." She took a little sip of air. *Almost there now.* "The surgeon – they had to call him to stop the bleeding – he said... He *said* I could never have another. Even if the seed took, I'd likely die in the attempt."

"So, they set you to net a werewolf. Because a werewolf cannot get you pregnant."

"See why I didn't fight it? One moment, one stupid, stupid choice, with one stupid man, and this becomes my only option."

"I become your only option."

She shook her head, desperate for him to understand.

"I still *wanted* something more, something better. Although I know I don't deserve it." Faith could feel her voice cracking, breath hitching. *I'll not cry any more this evening. Enough of that.*

"Not that I think I'm worth any form of loving. I just didn't want my existence to end as well, there, like that, with the baby. Do you see?"

"Oh, Lazuli." He tried to reach for her again. His face was pained and pulled into harsh lines. Ice cracked open under stress.

She held out her hands, palms forward – *wait*. This was like lancing a boil and she must pour out all her confessions like pus, ruining herself in his eyes forever. *I don't want your pity!*

"I wanted you. You know I wanted you. You were not a second choice, or my only option. You're glorious and perfect, and grumpy, and angry all the time, and secretive with your past. There are horrors there. I know there are. But it's different for you. It's different because you're a man. And you're immortal. And you have a pack. You still *have everything*. No matter what happened to you, don't you see how lucky you are?"

She looked down at her hands, struggling to keep the tears in. "And my baby *died*, bled out of me and taken away, stealing all my futures alongside. And I wanted you despite that, just a taste of what might have made it all worthwhile, do you see? Because I couldn't imagine *anything* after that. I couldn't imagine anything being good or kind or decent or whole ever again."

"Lazuli, I am none of those things."

She was fierce at him all of a sudden. Feeling her grief shift into something much easier to handle – rage, power, defence of that which she found worthy.

"No. You're not. You're not good or kind. You aren't decent or whole – but that's the point. Don't you see? I think we could be those things for each other. Us. Together." Her shoulders sagged. "Although I would understand now if, knowing all this, you don't want me anymore."

He snorted. A moment of his old arrogance, the tilting curl of a sneer that had first pulled her towards him.

"Wanting is not the problem, Lazuli." He cocked his head. "May I touch you now?"

She nodded.

He pulled her close and cradled her against him, and pressed his face hard into her neck, inhaling her scent. He did not kiss her. His hands were chaste even as they rubbed her back.

Faith had never felt such comfort.

STEP NINE

Small Tokens of Your Affection Are Always Welcome

Teddy interrupted them and there could be no more confessions that evening.

Faith and her cousin hailed a public conveyance to get home. Faith spent the drive vibrating with repressed wanting, and shared fears, and nerves too tight. She thought, slightly hysterically, that Channing might pluck out a tune upon her. He could once have been a musician, before he became a werewolf. All those with excess soul had gifts that must be given up with the bite; what had Channing sacrificed? Too much, she suspected.

Faith felt purged and free, empty and weak, and terribly needy. She was so many things all at once, it was a wonder she did not collapse.

Fortunately, Teddy somehow understood. She sat close and clutched one of Faith's hands in both of hers. Silent for a change. Faith wondered at that; in all their months of intimacy, she had never known Teddy to be silent for more than five minutes together.

At home, Teddy shepherded Faith upstairs and saw

her delivered safely into Minnie's worried care.

"I will explain everything to Mums," said Teddy, closing the door behind her.

Faith wondered what that meant, exactly, and what form such an explanation might take.

"Oh, miss," said Minnie, "you look awful."

Faith gave a dry chuckle.

Minnie also looked somewhat shaken. She moved awkwardly and her cap was pulled full forward over her head, so it shadowed her eyes. Maybe she, too, had been crying, or was exhausted and overworked.

"I'm fine, Minnie dear, a little upset by some things that happened tonight and definitely ready for bed. Are you all right?"

"Yes, miss, just tired." Minnie began to help her with her dress. Her hands shook a little.

"Minnie, are you sure? You can tell me anything, you know. I won't judge. And I'll help you in any way I can."

"I shouldn't, miss, not when you've had a bad night yourself, but I'm sorry, I have to tell you something."

Faith suddenly remembered before the gallery, what her mother had said. "I should warn you. Mother is looking for you. She's annoyed about you working for a seamstress. I don't know why. She might come to see you tomorrow. Unfortunately."

"I know, miss. That's what I'm trying to tell you."

"Never say she tracked you down already? She must have gone straight to yell at you after yelling at me. I'm so sorry."

"No miss, not her. Your father found me."

Faith was utterly flummoxed. "Papa? But why? You mean he came to see you, at the modiste? What…"

It made no sense. Papa had never set foot in a

modiste's in his life. He didn't involve himself in the domestic running of a household. What on earth was he doing, tracking down Faith's maid in her secondary place of business?

"Please, miss. Just let me speak. If I get it all out now, then maybe I'll actually say it all. But if you interrupt me..."

Faith nodded, eyes wide, mouth firmly closed. *An evening for confessions, I see.*

Faith had her nightgown on now and was sitting on the edge of the bed while Minnie paced in front of her in nervous agitation.

"Miss, did you know my father was killed by vampires?"

Faith shook her head.

"During the war. He fought for the Union and didn't make it back. They found him, drained and punctured. It forced me into service. Before he died, he earned enough for me not to have to work. But after..."

Faith nodded again. Ashamed she had never asked about her maid's circumstances. She knew some of the generalities but not the particulars.

Minnie took a deep breath and blurted, "Your mother came to me with a task. She gave me something and asked me to deliver it, well, *them*, to a business associate of your father's here in London. Anti-vampire, she said."

Minnie lifted her sewing kit then. Faith knew it well; she herself had given it to Minnie several years earlier. It was one of the hatbox-shaped models, designed for high-end seamstresses. It had special extra-sharp scissors in varying sizes, a fancy iron (one of the self-steaming models), and all the best micro-gadgets to come out of the European domestic service inventors over the past decade. It hadn't come cheap, but Faith knew how much Minnie loved to sew.

"Your tool kit?"

Minnie nodded and set it on the floor to pop it open, lifting out the accordion shelves. It was constructed like a sewing basket but modified heavily to specific technologies. It had lots of nooks and crannies to stash both gadgets and supplies and was Minnie's pride and joy. It also had a hidden compartment that only Minnie, Faith, and the original maker knew about.

Minnie popped open this secret drawer and pulled out what looked to be two or three dozen tiny bobbins, each one loosely wound with yarn.

Minnie handed one to Faith to look over.

The yarn was clearly a disguise, because the small bobbin was far too heavy to be a real bobbin, and not shaped at all correctly upon close inspection. Faith pulled off the yarn. Underneath, it looked like an elaborately filigreed version of...

"A bullet?"

Minnie nodded. "Sundowner bullets."

Faith gasped and dropped the deadly little thing onto the bed. "Oh, Minnie."

Faith stared down at it, innocently resting on her coverlet, horrified. There before her was the only thing that could reliably kill a vampire or a werewolf. It was the standard brass color of most bullets (not that Faith had a great of familiarity with projectiles), only this one was pretty and jewelry-like – caged, patterned, and cored with threads of grey and shards of blond. Incredibly expensive and complicated to produce, a Sundowner bullet incorporated both silver and rowan wood, yet could be loaded and shot like any other .36 caliber.

Sundowner armaments were strictly patented and production was tightly controlled, even more so in England than in the Union. In fact, only a few people in all of Britain were authorized to use them, let alone make them, and most of those were supernaturals themselves.

Faith suddenly knew. "Major Channing was looking for these, wasn't he, when he pulled aside my specimen case? I thought it was his fierceness that scared you, but you had these with you all along. That's why you were so nervous."

Minnie nodded. "Yes, miss. Lucky for me, the higher the rank, the more likely they are to forget servants are people, not property or furniture."

Faith winced. "I take it you failed to deliver to Papa's associate. Why?"

Minnie grimaced. "I thought I could sell 'em myself. Turn a tidy profit, use the money to emigrate to Europe. I didn't know how hard it is to fence bullets in a foreign land, especially when one is only a lady's maid."

"Did you take the work with Mrs Honeybun in an effort to pursue this illicit activity?"

Minnie hung her head. "Yes, miss, in part. I mean, I do like it. The money from the sale would have gone into me starting my own dress shop. But it's too hard for someone like me to sell something like this. I've never done it before, miss. Please believe me."

Faith could understand wanting independence. She could understand hating the supernatural set. She didn't blame Minnie.

"We're all sinners, Minnie, in some form or another. But why confess now?"

"Your father wants his bullets back. And he didn't ask nicely."

Minnie pushed at her cap, revealing what she'd been hiding under it. One of her eyes was dark and swollen. She'd clearly been beaten.

"Mrs Honeybun yelled for lawmen and he ran. But he'll return."

Faith nodded. "You're safe here tonight, I think. The Iftercasts have taken against my parents, thank heavens. I don't know what we did to deserve the care of such nice people, Minnie."

"True, miss."

Faith patted the counterpane, and Minnie put the bullets away and came to sit next to her. Still trembling a little.

"And tomorrow, miss, what then?"

"Did you hear that I'm engaged, Minnie?"

"No, miss. Felicitations?"

"To a werewolf."

"The grumpy one from after we landed, who you yelled at?"

"Yes, Minnie, that's him."

Minnie gave a small smile that might have been approval. "Very good, miss."

Faith said, "Here's what I think we should do…"

Channing believed that Biffy would come to talk to him about his hasty choices, but it was Lyall who found him.

Channing was in the library of Falmouth House, his favorite haunt when he must be at home. Which wasn't often but, he supposed, with a wife, might become more frequent in the future. He'd claimed one of the small tables for his desk, and most of the rest of the pack left him be. Children were not allowed in the library. Not until they could actually read.

He was examining a set of shelves in the brightest corner of the room. Or what would be the brightest corner, with the curtains open and the sun above the horizon.

The shelves were sparsely populated with only the cheapest of volumes. Book spines were too likely to fade on these particular shelves, since the staff had orders to open all the downstairs windows in the summertime and to draw the curtains year 'round. Just because werewolves could only be awake at night did not mean they allowed a gloomy, cheerless, stuffy habitat like that of the vampires.

After long consideration, Channing began removing those few books that were on the shelves and rehoming them elsewhere in the library.

The London Pack didn't boast a particularly vast book collection. In fact, it might be called embarrassingly petite. Channing thought that he ought to put a concerted effort into improving it. It had dwindled considerably since he joined the pack. Most of the political, historical, and technical manuals had migrated to BUR over the last half century. A great many books had been abandoned by the pack in the library at Woolsey Castle when they'd been forced to relocate to London. They were now the property of the resident vampires. Once a hive got their fangs into something, it was easier to buy another than demand it back.

"What are you doing, Channing? Cataloging?" Professor Lyall came into the room.

"Oh, it's you. No, reorganizing."

Lyall watched him for a moment. "You have plans for those now-empty shelves?"

"I do." Channing was churlish. "I trust you don't object, Beta?"

"Depends on the plans."

Channing did not answer the unasked question. "Lyall, what do you want?"

"I understand you have sealed the deal with Miss Wigglesworth."

"Faith. Yes. You've come to put me off?"

"Certainly not. Biffy approves. You know the rest of the pack all like her very much. Those who have met her, at least. I think she'll fit in well here. And we will, of course, look after her should you run away."

"You think that likely, do you?"

"The odds favor it."

"You haven't much faith in me."

"Channing, I've known you for a hundred years, give or take a decade. You've never kept a woman for more than a few hours, let alone the span of a mortal lifetime. Frankly, I do not know what to expect. Up until this moment, you were nothing if not predictable in your loneliness."

"She needs us rather badly."

"Yes, I know. It does not have to be you who marries her."

"Yes, it does." Channing's lip curled and he bared his teeth.

Lyall rolled his eyes at this display of possessiveness. "You're sure you're good enough for her?"

"Most assuredly not. But she seems to think so, and I want to try for her sake."

Lyall gave a tight little sigh. "Channing, you must tell

her about Odette."

"I know."

"And Isolde."

"Don't say that name."

Lyall stood before him then, stopping him from pacing and fiddling with books and shelves.

Channing nearly walked right into him.

Lyall didn't flinch – small, sandy-haired, self-effacing and urbane, infinitely powerful. A great deal stronger than Channing in every way. His enemy, his friend, his stabilization over the decades. There was so much time shared between them that they had become two thirds of a whole. Two thirds unchanging over the course of three Alphas now.

Channing remembered his howler training from when he'd first been metamorphosed. He thought on it often. The balance of the pack, the rule of three. Alpha for the head, evolving, shifting, holding too many tethers, burning brighter than the rest of the pack until he snuffed himself out in madness. Beta for the heart, beating a steady rhythm of care, love, resilience, ever steadfast. Gamma for the strength in arms, the warrior, the challenger, the weapon, to remind the pack of what they really were – hunters, trackers, fighters. To remind them to survive first.

Lyall stepped close, placed his hands to either side of Channing's face, and breathed with him. Beta calm. Balance and focus. *Lyall – my opposite in all things.* What the Beta gives to the pack, the Gamma takes away. Challenge to support, fight to acceptance, peace for a time, until challenge comes again. The cycle of the wolf.

"Channing." His Beta's voice was mellow. "If she is in love with you, and I think she is – although you can't have made it easy for her, poor little thing – then she deserves to know all of you."

Channing could not deny this. Faith had spread herself raw and tenderized before him this very evening, cut herself open like fresh meat. He had craved her before he knew all her story, and now? Now he hungered for her, ravenous, and it was just possible he loved her a little. Even a lot. Which was truly terrifying.

"If you want to keep her for yourself – and I think you *need* to keep her – she has a right to know all of it."

The next day, during early evening visiting hours, no one was surprised to see Mrs Iftercast, Miss Iftercast, and Miss Wigglesworth call upon the werewolves of Falmouth House. Or, to be precise, since the sun was not yet down, they were visiting the daylight support staff and clavigers of Falmouth House.

Everyone had heard the wildly romantic and mildly horrific story of the gallery the night before. More important, it was now understood and officially reported that Miss Wigglesworth had netted herself a werewolf. The fact that it was Major Channing was a surprise only to those who had not been watching his deranged courtship of her over the past few months.

Those who had, nodded wisely and said that while it might have looked peculiar from the outside, the major was an old-fashioned type, and perhaps it was a werewolf courting ritual of some seventy years gone. The very old (the howlers, the record-keepers, and the vampires) wondered about Major Channing's first wife. But they did not say anything, because they were also old enough to know when to hold their tongues.

The fact that little Miss Wigglesworth brought her maid along with her to call at Falmouth House was thought a trifle odd. Suggestions were made that this was, most likely, an American custom. Others thought perhaps she intended to inspect the household and the running thereof, and that the maid would provide assistance in the matter of downstairs staff. Miss Wigglesworth would be the first proper wife to enter the London Pack since Lady Maccon. It was expected that she would take over the running of day-to-day concerns (or night-to-night, as it were). Of course, she would wish to visit during daylight hours if she wanted to meet the children and see the clavigers.

Faith and Minnie hid in the safety of the pack house until after sunset.

Whether her parents would try to get ahold of either of them was a moot point. Falmouth House did not open its doors to just anyone, visiting hours or not. After all, during the daytime, the pack had no one high enough ranked awake to receive. Also, in England it was not done, as a general rule, to call upon werewolves; one waited for them to call upon you.

Faith and Teddy had a very pleasant time of it. They played with the two children, gossiped with the clavigers (a cheerful, rowdy bunch who nevertheless tried to put on a few airs and graces in the presence of ladies). Faith had her work cut out for her with them – actors and opera singers and such. She enjoyed the challenge. Mrs Iftercast knitted and watched them all indulgently (no doubt imagining her own future grandchildren) while Minnie paced and tried not to look nervous.

The children were sweet. Robbie was a dear little fellow with a perpetual smile. He sat on Teddy's lap, cooing and drooling in the manner of most small infants. Occasionally, he emitted a garbled word or two. Gracie played on the floor with Mrs Whybrew. Mrs Whybrew was a frank, chatty female whom Faith instantly liked. She seemed to have developed a certain adaptive pattern of habits, or possibly pseudo-supernatural abilities, being the only female in the household. Well, her and Gracie. Faith hoped they could be friends; they would likely need to form an alliance.

An hour or so after sunset, as was right and proper, Lord Falmouth descended the staircase and entered his drawing room with both hands extended in welcome.

"Miss Wigglesworth, delighted to find you here!" Biffy drew her forwards to bestow a kiss upon either cheek in a manner that young people adopted after visiting Europe.

Very modern, thought Faith, pleased by the familial intimacy.

"I cannot tell you how happy I am to officially welcome you to my home as a soon-to-be pack member. Things couldn't have turned out better. Really, they couldn't. I am so very pleased."

Faith blushed and wanted to hug him but thought maybe that was taking things too far. *We might get there eventually,* she hoped. The werewolves seemed a physically affectionate lot. Always bumping into each other and throwing arms about shoulders.

Biffy grinned. "Have you come to inspect the place? I assure you Lyall runs a tight ship. Although he'll be delighted to shunt some of the household burdens onto you. He is eager to resume the full scope of his former duties at BUR. Were you aware that he was once an investigator with them?"

Faith shook her had. "I thought Major Channing..."

"Ah, no, Channing took over from Lord Maccon. Lyall held the secondary position, but he has been away these twenty years and his post has remained vacant. The two of them have already departed for Fleet Street, as a matter of fact. First thing this evening out the back of the house. Didn't smell you here, I'm afraid. Terrible hurry. Something to do with Channing's current case. It's giving him some stick. Lyall has an excellent nose, you know?"

Minnie gave a little squeak.

Biffy's attention shifted to her. "And who have we here?"

"This is my maid, Minnie. I'm sorry to say we need to speak to Major Channing right away."

"Ah, the eager bride."

Faith tried to give Biffy a significant look that neither Teddy nor Mrs Iftercast could see. "It is a matter of urgent business. Very *particular* business."

Biffy looked impressed. "Oh, is it, indeed? My, but you are full of surprises, lovely Faith. *Urgent,* you say? Well, if you will allow some of the other pack to entertain you, I'll go fetch him back myself. I could use a run. It's getting on towards full moon, we all get a little restless about this time of the month. But we will tell you all about that sort of thing later. Don't want to keep you waiting."

Biffy was clearly eager to hear her information but guessed that she'd speak only to Channing.

He bowed himself out of the drawing room. As if this were some sort of signal, Mr Quinn, Mr Ditmarsh, and Mr Hemming came in. Quinn and Hemming clearly wanted some time with the pack's children before they were put to bed.

Quinn lifted Robbie up out of Teddy's lap and swung him high. The boy squealed in delight.

"How's my little man?" He buried his face in Robbie's round tummy and made a steam engine noise.

Robbie shrieked in laughter.

Hemming scooped up Gracie and took her on a *dirigible float*, as he called it. This involved Gracie lying splayed on his stretched-out arms while he bobbed about the room, making a whooshing noise.

Mrs Whybrew said to Faith, "Aren't they ridiculous?"

Faith said, "I think it's adorable."

Mr Ditmarsh came to stand next to them, shaking his head. "Big, fearsome werewolf brutes indeed. Should this get out, the pack's reputation would be in ruins."

Faith and Teddy both grinned.

Mr Ditmarsh looked at them in all seriousness. "Miss Wigglesworth, Miss Iftercast, we depend upon you not to breathe a word of this to anyone."

Teddy and Faith exchanged amused nods.

"We will take it to the grave," vowed Faith.

Teddy giggled as Hemming and Gracie bobbed by her.

Mrs Whybrew rolled her eyes. "Oh, now, boys! Don't you go an' rile them up so afore bed. Get along now, take the ladies away and feed them. Leave me to my business, do!"

At the nanny's insistence, the gentlemen put the babies down and filed out, leading Faith and her cousins into the dining room.

There, Faith and the Iftercasts sipped tea and nibbled bread-and-butter sandwiches while the werewolves, and those few clavigers still around, ate vast quantities of roast mutton and chopped liver on toast and tried not to be too bawdy, although it was clearly a trial for them.

Faith was in heaven. It was fun. They were fun.

Minnie stayed with the children in the guise of helping put them to bed. Faith hoped that her keeping busy would put her mind at ease. It wasn't entirely effective; Minnie eventually slipped into the dining hall to stand in one corner, clutching her sewing tool kit and watching the raucous werewolves with wide, fearful eyes.

Teddy stretched over at one point to grab the butter, almost across Mr Zev, who was leaning far back in his chair in order to throw a roll at Mr Bluebutton for being "that much more of a pompous twig than usual." Teddy's own breach of etiquette was wholly disregarded (except by her mother, who glared and hissed, "Theodora, resume your proper seat this instant!").

Another bun flew across the table at Zev and missed Teddy only because she lurched aside to hiss at Faith, "Do you think this is what goes on at a gentlemen's club? Oh, would you look at Mums! She doesn't know whether to laugh or cry. I guess they were very much on their best behavior when we were all here for dinner before."

Faith swallowed down a grin. "Either that or the absence of the three top-ranking wolves leaves a vacancy in proper conduct."

"Oh, do you think? Of course. That is possible."

Mr Ditmarsh gave them a wink.

Oops, thought Faith, *supernatural hearing, I forgot.*

"Sadly, ladies, we are always like this. Lyall threatened us with turnips for a week if we didn't behave when you first dined with us."

"We hate turnips." Hemming grabbed the next flying roll right out of the air and took a huge bite out of it.

"To a man," added Quinn.

"*To a wolf,* shouldn't it be?" wondered Faith.

At which juncture the door to the dining room burst open, although from where Faith was sitting, she couldn't see anything come through it.

Then Minnie screamed as if she were being murdered.

Faith saw his tail first, white and fluffy; it swayed back and forth like a banner. Then a massive wolf trotted around the table and stalked directly towards her.

She barely noticed there were two other wolves behind him, both smaller, one dark, one light.

But this wolf was magnificent – pure white, enormous but lean, a true predator. His eyes were icy blue and his pink tongue lolled out one side of his mouth, panting. He must have run very fast to get back to her so quickly.

He trotted to Faith and without pause placed his saucer-sized front paws, most likely dirty from running the streets of London, onto the side of her chair and stood up.

He leaned forward and pressed his head into her neck and huffed at her.

Which was when Faith unfroze. It was not that she'd been afraid, only that she had prey instincts exactly like any other human. Here was a wolf, hunter, and if Mr Darwin was to be believed, somewhere inside her, way back, was a monkey, small and afraid. All she had been able to think, for those first few moments, was that she was sitting in the dining room and a wolf was charging at her. But now she realized who that wolf was.

"Good evening, Channing." A new instinct kicked in, that of beloved, and Faith twisted in her chair to bury both her hands in his thick fur. It managed to be both soft and coarse at the same time, and it was very warm and lush.

"You got here quickly. Did you hear that I brought you a present? A sort of engagement gift." She didn't know if he could understand her when he was a wolf. He'd mentioned something once about not being entirely himself when he was in his shifted form. But he must have some level of intelligence, for he clearly recognized her.

She pushed back from the table and stood. He pressed against her side, almost herding her, separating her from the rest of the men in the room.

She allowed it, resting her hand on his head as he led her through and away from the others into the hallway.

A squeak of horror gave her pause.

Minnie had followed them, barely breathing, almost petrified with fear. It was one thing to know that werewolves existed; it was another to be confronted by incontrovertible proof.

"Join us, please, Minnie." Faith tried to sound encouraging.

The wolf growled.

"Now, now, Channing, Minnie is instrumental in this. She has your gift."

Minnie whispered. "Please, miss, don't make me."

Faith closed her eyes briefly and sighed. "Give them to me, then."

Minnie delved into her tool kit and handed over the velvet drawstring bag in which they'd stashed the bullets. Faith had to lean forward and grab them from her maid, as the wolf, teeth bared, stood between them.

Minnie turned and fled the house.

Faith wondered if she would ever see her again.

Channing nudged her towards the back of the hall, stopping expectantly in front of a large and imposing door.

"In here?"

He chuffed at her. He really was a particularly fine-looking wolf, with that lovely white coat and those beautiful blue eyes. Faith didn't find him fearsome in the least, now that she was accustomed to the idea.

A little hesitant – after all, this was not her house, not yet, at any road – Faith opened the door and pushed into the room.

It appeared that this was the pack library. Faith instantly adored it. The room was generously proportioned with bookshelves against practically every wall. There was space for a large fireplace in one corner. Here and there stood a small table or a desk, or a cluster of comfortable looking leather chairs and couches.

There were not a great many books. Faith remembered that the pack had only recently moved to Falmouth House. She wondered if they would let her add her own books to the collection. She hadn't managed to bring many with her from America, only her favorite mineral identification manuals and geological treatises. She thought maybe Channing would let her buy more and expand the library further. Her husband-to-be seemed utterly unperturbed by her unladylike scientific pursuits. She wondered if he might even encourage her in them. He'd courted her with gifts of rocks, after all. Suddenly, she had a million questions for him, about domestic arrangements, about her future, about their future together, in this house with this pack. There were so many possibilities. So much she needed to know.

"Would you change back into a human for me, please?" she begged the wolf.

The wolf only chuffed and led her to the far side of the room, where a beautiful bay window stuck out. There were thick, heavy curtains to keep out the sunlight. This was the house of immortals, after all. But behind the curtains, the window boasted a cushioned seat and a beautiful view of Blackheath under the stars. Faith instantly imagined spending many a rainy evening curled there reading, a crackling fire in the hearth, and a white wolf asleep at her feet, or a tall blond man with a snobbish expression cuddling her close.

"Oh!" said Faith. "It's perfect."

The wolf woofed at her, softly, and seemed to want her attention on some empty shelves nearby.

"You know, I could understand you better if you spoke actual words." She stroked him, running her hands through the thick fur, tracing the wolf bones underneath, marveling that he could transition between the two. She played with the velvety softness of his ears and he trembled against her in pleasure, massive tail wagging back and forth, hitting a puffy hassock behind him with a rhythmic thumping.

She looked into his blue eyes. Exactly the same ice blue as when he was a man. "You're so beautiful," she told the wolf and the man, in case he was in there, hidden behind the eyes. "Come back to me now, please, Channing?"

He stepped away from her with another one of those pleasant chuffing noises.

Then the noises became entirely unpleasant. Faith winced at the sound of breaking bones and shifting flesh. Her eyes welling with sympathetic tears, she watched, both horrified and fascinated, as the white wolf shifted. He transitioned smoothly from beast to man, but it was no doubt an agony. His white fur seemed to crawl along his body towards his head as the man emerged. Fur became hair, snout shortened to nose, blue eyes bled into bigger blue, pointed velvet ears shrank down, becoming small, round, and human.

There was a dimorphic moment when Faith believed the wolf was the real Channing and the man was merely a temporary manifestation of the beast. She wanted the wolf back because she knew that form comforted him. But that was pure fancy; he was both, and neither.

Finally, he stood before her, all pale skin and long lean muscles, tall and lanky, and fit and very naked.

STEP TEN

Get Him to the Altar

"Oh!" Faith slapped her hands up to cover her eyes, knowing her cheeks must be pink.

Channing, the cad, gave a low laugh. "Don't you enjoy the view, Lazuli? One would think you might like to approve the goods before you purchased, so to speak."

Faith had only ever seen one fully naked man before. To be fair, she had found Kit nice to look upon. Now she thought him much less aesthetically pleasing than Major Channing, but she'd always liked how different the male form was from her own.

She peeked through her fingertips.

Channing was standing before her, unashamed, arms crossed, expression sardonically amused.

"I suppose I should get used to it, living among werewolves." Still peeking.

He glared. "I should prefer that it be me you looked at, as a general rule."

Faith dropped her hands and glared at him – determinedly only his face. "I promise, sir, I've no interest elsewhere!"

He grinned. "Good. You are mine now."

"And you're mine. Which means no changing shape in front of just any lady in a library! Or any other place, either."

Faith wanted it understood that his philandering days were over.

His lips twitched. "So, my Lazuli, would you like to tell me why Biffy dragged me back from my work this evening when I had barely arrived? Not that I'm not delighted to see you at any given opportunity, but surely it could wait a little?"

"You really want to have this conversation right now?"

"You wanted me."

"But you haven't any clothes on!"

"One might hope that would make you want me more."

Faith snorted. Then, feeling very brazen, she allowed her gaze to travel over him. He was pleasingly shaped. Everything about him was *more* than Kit – more muscle and height, more presence and attention. He was focused wholly on her. She wanted to touch. To run her hands over his chest, which was oddly hairless, and over his hips and down, following the V of muscles to where…

Well, there you have it. That, too, is more. She thought it was likely a strange thing to find *that* part of his anatomy also aesthetically pleasing, but she did.

She stared. "Is that because of me?"

He huffed. "I want you rather badly, Lazuli. You doubted that?"

"It's impressive."

He laughed. "Words every man everywhere wishes to hear. It's adequate to the task. Have you looked your fill?"

"You aren't going to do anything about it?"

"I have some control. Give me a little credit. I need not take you here, bent over the couch in the pack library like an animal… Oh, you *like* that idea, do you?"

Faith hadn't even realized she'd whimpered. Her whole body felt suddenly flushed, itching and needy. The image was wicked and arousing. She wondered what he would do if she lifted up her skirts and pulled aside her combinations and offered to do exactly what he described.

He stepped in close to her. "Look at your eyes," he breathed. "So big and dark."

A funny growling-yipping noise interrupted them.

A smaller wolf trotted into the room, his tail waving madly. He was dark brown in color with oxblood markings about his neck and chest that made him look as though he were wearing a scarf. He was dragging something along with his mouth, hence the funny noise.

Faith whirled to place herself defensively in front of Channing's naked form.

The wolf spat out the cloth in his mouth and yipped again, clearly laughing at them.

"Biffy?" guessed Faith.

"Oh, shove off, Alpha," said Channing.

Biffy growled at him.

"Yes, I'll be good."

Biffy bent and nosed the piece of clothing he'd been carrying. Faith thought it must be a dressing gown or a robe of some kind.

"Yes, yes, I'll put it on. Although it's covered in wolf slobber now. Thank you very much."

The wolf stuck his nose in the air in an offended

manner that suggested the mere idea that he would *ever* slobber on *any* item of clothing, least of all a dressing gown, was absurd. Then he turned and pranced haughtily from the room. He kicked the door closed casually with a back foot as he left.

Channing bent, reached around Faith, and pulled on the dressing gown, tying it about his waist with a sash. It was too short, particularly in the arms, and tight over his shoulders, suggesting it was, in fact, Biffy's dressing gown. It was made of a fine quilted emerald-green satin.

Faith was disappointed. Although it would be easier to think coherently now he was covered up.

"Shall we begin again?" suggested Channing. "How are you this evening, my Lazuli?" He bent and kissed her, chaste and sweet, although she could feel his interest against her stomach. This made her squirm against him.

He chuckled. "Yes, exactly so, but I believe you had a matter of some urgency to discuss with me?"

Faith nodded, took a breath, and backed away to present him with the velvet bag.

He opened it, curious, and dipped a hand inside to pull out one of the bullets.

"Well, I never. How on earth?"

There was no accusation in his tone. He trusted her. He simply had no idea how she'd come by the Sundowner bullets he'd been looking for.

"Minnie, my maid, had them all along."

"Your maid? Ah, the one who screamed when I came in."

"You remember that?"

"I remember everything from when I am a wolf. I simply cannot control myself in quite the same way."

"Do you understand me when I speak to you?"

He nodded.

"Good to know. Well, Minnie was given them by my father to bring to London for one of his associates. It's all wrapped up in some anti-supernatural agenda, I'm sure. You probably know more than I on the reasoning and intended distribution. This being your territory and all."

He inclined his head. "And how does your marrying one of us fit into your father's schemes?"

Faith shrugged. "I honestly believe they think of me as a curse upon you, or a punishment. That horrible scene at the gallery was meant to humiliate and embarrass you as well as me. This way, they punish us both. Me for shaming them, and you for being a werewolf. They think… well, they *think* you love me, and so it would be crushing for you to find out the truth."

"I *do* love you," he said, so softly she barely heard it.

Faith was already soldiering on. "Minnie kept them instead, tried to sell them herself. Please don't be angry. She only wanted the money to make her own way. But she couldn't find a buyer, so she told me everything, doing the right thing in the end, I suppose. I brought them to you as a kind of engagement present. They're what you were looking for all along, aren't they?"

"Turns out I was looking for you."

"You're being sweet to me. I don't know what to do when you're sweet."

"I shall go back to being a cad momentarily."

"So, it's all fine? With the bullets, I mean."

"Hang the bullets."

"But I thought you wanted them."

"I did, I do, and I'm glad to have them turn up at last. But hush a moment, Lazuli, I have something I must say to you."

Silence descended for a long time while he looked at her oddly. It was as if he were gathering his courage before some military action. Turning into a soldier before her eyes – shifting forms again. Channing, who never seemed afraid of anything, was terrified of something he must say to her.

Faith hesitated and then put her hand out, resting it on the lapel of his robe. "You brought me into the library for some particular reason?"

"Oh, yes, that." He tilted his head down, like a naughty schoolboy. "I thought, perhaps, these here, for you." He gestured casually behind himself with one hand.

Faith blinked; there was nothing there other than empty shelves. "They're very nice shelves, but is this your library to give?"

Channing chuckled, embarrassed. "Ah, yes, I mean to say, the *space* on the shelves." He came over all gruff when he was embarrassed; it was cute. "For your rock collection? The, erm, minerals and such. We could line the shelves with velvet if you like? Put glass doors over the front. Anything you think necessary."

"Oh!" said Faith, and then again. "Oh." She looked at the shelves reverently with new eyes. "They're *beautiful*."

He snorted. "They are only shelves."

She whirled on him. "How dare you be so perfect?"

She could see her rocks there. She only had enough, right now, for one small corner, lined in black satin maybe, to showcase them in all their simple beauty. She might make up little white labels; maybe someone in the pack knew calligraphy. Then, during the day, when everyone else was asleep, she could open the curtains and look at them under the sunlight.

"And you'll take me into the countryside collecting?" She asked this even knowing she wanted too much, but unable to resist.

"I will. And I will sleep in a tiny cottage while you and whatever poor Iftercast cousin you have recruited to your cause go tramping about, chiseling away at things all day. When they are older, you will no doubt take Robbie and Gracie with you."

Faith pushed for more. *I'm always so demanding.* "I want to see Dover."

"It is very picturesque."

"The white cliffs."

"Of course it is the cliffs you want."

"And the red clay further south."

"I will take you to see clay, my heart."

"Oh." Faith clasped her hands. "This is *so romantic*."

Channing rolled his eyes and snorted. "I give her clay and empty shelves and she is in ecstasies."

"And I'll come home wet from wandering the moors and curl up against you as the sun sets, and you'll wake to find me there next to you."

"Now who is being romantic?"

Faith remembered something he'd said earlier, when she was tumbling over her words, confessing Minnie's sins. "You love me!"

"Now she listens," he grumbled to himself.

"But that's *wonderful*."

"No, my Lazuli, it's not."

"But I love you."

"I know."

"That's not a very nice response."

"My sweet, I have loved before and it went badly for me. I'm afraid my loving you will go badly for you."

She was staunch in her defence of him. "Never!"

He sighed. "You do not know the half of it."

Channing shook his head. She really was a most aggravating female when she set her mind to something – how could he not adore her?

"Sit down a moment, please, Lazuli, and let me try to explain. It's not easy. This is not a topic I enjoy discussing."

Faith nodded and he knew she understood. She'd not wanted to talk about her lost child and neither did he. In this, they were alike. Yet she'd mustered the courage to do so, and he owed her for that. Plus, he couldn't let one small mortal female outmatch him in bravery.

Faith said nothing, only looked at him with wide blue eyes, sympathetic and patient. She crossed her white hands in her lap and sat in the bay window exactly as he had imagined her. He wanted to return to wolf form and lie at her feet; things were so much simpler when he was a beast. She would run those small hands though his fur, lightly, reverently, as she had only moments before.

He had to chase that future if he truly wanted it. He had to earn it.

"I was a sculptor before the bite. Not a particularly good or famous one, although I might have become so, given a different life. I lived in Paris for a time, there is – was – a great sculptor there, Pajou. You've heard of him?"

Faith shook her head.

"It was a long time ago. I was barely twenty when I met Odette. She was so beautiful. This fair, frail creature with flaming hair and big green eyes. I loved her rather madly, as only the young can really love. We married and had a child."

He paused, gathering his courage. A name he had hadn't spoken in decades. "Isolde was this bright, vibrant little fairy girl. So much energy and life. Odette was not a good mother, always sickly and sad. I suppose, initially, I was attracted to the darkness in her – this tortured soul appealed to the artist in me. She spent a great deal of time in bed after Isolde was born. So, it was mainly the two of us, father and daughter. I would have Isolde with me in the studio while I worked."

Faith held still, barely breathing, eyes big and fierce on his face – as if she might hold him together with her will alone.

He thought he was doing well so far. His voice was firm. His delivery crisp. "We were so young. I thought Odette would change. And she did improve a little. She began to eat more, smile occasionally. Sometimes, she even touched Isolde, like a mother ought. But then Napoleon happened. At first, he had so little effect on us. A poor artist and his family, even a British one living in Paris, knows so very little of politics and armies. But you feel it when a country goes to war, even if you aren't facing it directly. The whole place catches fever, like marsh sickness. Still, I thought we would be fine. I thought: *it's Paris*. We had this little apartment on the bank of the Seine – the bedroom window opened out over the water. I thought, if anything, the danger would come from outside, from my own country's invasion, and then

I would merely claim to be British and all would be well."

Now comes the difficult part. "Isolde was three when the vampires tried to recruit me. The hives—" He paused, took a breath. "The hives in France, they don't obey the same rules as here in England. They still don't legally exist. Back then, they were barely tolerated, living on the fringes of society, preying on blood whores. They waved immortality in front of artists, much as they do here, but drones had no safety via patronage or indenture. Apparently, they'd been watching me, and they knew I had artistic skill. I refused, of course. I had Odette and Isolde to consider. Vampires don't like to be refused."

Channing sat down at that, abruptly, and looked at his hands, trying to get his words in order. It was too much to sit next to her, so he chose an armchair nearby instead.

Faith, bless her, said nothing, merely continued to watch him, curious and supportive and loving.

I hope that look does not change. Please don't let it change.

"The war was in earnest and everything was in chaos. No one was watching the vampires. No one was hunting them anymore. The Templars were off killing mortals for a change. This one queen, well, she really wanted me, and so she took me. Right off the street when I was out trying to find bread. She kept me trapped in her rooms. Feeding off me, trying to get me to – you know – although *that* a man can refuse to do. It wasn't very long. At least, I don't think it was. A month, perhaps, maybe two. But it was long enough for Odette."

He paused, worried about how best to say this worst bit.

"She waited for me, you see. Even though she'd lost all faith in me. Perhaps she thought I'd abandoned her and returned to England. Or perhaps she'd word that I was still in Paris, being kept by a vampire queen, and thought I'd volunteered. But she waited for me to return. So she could look me in the eyes when she jumped."

Faith gasped and closed her own eyes. "I'm so sorry. It's not your fault, it's not—"

He interrupted her, slogging on. "She took Isolde with her. Right out the window and into the Seine. I wasn't fast enough to stop her. I dove in after, but I never found them. I never found either of them. And Paris was burning."

Faith looked at him with such sympathetic eyes. He knew she understood what held him back from her, from trusting a woman. She said the only thing she could. "It is not the same, but I do know what it is to lose a child."

He nodded.

"What did you do?"

He gave a pained smile. "I left Paris for London, joined the Coldsteam Guards as a raw recruit – a fathead artist who'd never held a gun. I fought three wars, ended up in Iberia under the Fifth Coalition. Caught the eyes of the Alpha of the regiment's allied pack. Lord Vulkasin thought I had such fire in my blood. He didn't know I simply didn't care about dying. He found out I used to sculpt. So, when the bullet came that should have killed me and it was a nighttime rush near to full moon, he offered me the bite. I took it. I thought letting go of most of my soul would make everything better for my heart. Turns out it simply makes everything harder."

Her eyes were earnest on his face, willing him to go on.

"Werewolves, we may be undead, but we feel just as much. We love just as deeply, but it's right there under our skin. It's closer, more vibrant, lodged into flesh and bone rather than heart. It hurts, all the time, whatever you feel, even love, simply *hurts*. So, I gave it all up."

Faith tilted her head. "You had another reason for taking the bite, didn't you?"

How can she already know me so well, after so short an acquaintance?

He nodded. "Revenge. After the wars ended, I returned to Paris and killed the vampire queen who'd kidnapped me. It took some planning." He gave what he knew was a toothy smile. "I allowed her to trap me, cage me, treat me like a dog. I bided my time for one small slip. Stupidly, she kept me in her inner chamber, where she slept. Her pet, she called me. I still" – he paused, shivering – "cannot bear to be called *dog*."

Faith's voice was soft and fervent. "I will *never* do so."

He'd handed her a weapon and she'd turned it into a vow.

"She did slip one evening, as I knew she would. Full moon and she didn't bar the cage properly. Foolish vampire. Deadly mistake, as it turned out. I ripped her head off. Not easy with a queen. They taste awful and their skin is quite tough."

Faith looked pale but composed. "Go on."

"The hive swarmed and went mad with bloodlust. They rampaged through Paris, killing hundreds. France abolished vampires as a result. I hadn't thought of that, you see? I only thought of my revenge. I didn't know what would happen. How awful they would be. How many innocents would die. But I'm also not sure I wouldn't do it again."

Her eyes showed no judgment.

"I went wild and loner after that. Lived as a wolf most nights, slept the days in caves in the deep forest. Took myself away from everything. I think, in some parts of Europe, they still tell stories of the white wolf after the war."

"What happened? What brought you back?"

"Lyall."

"Ah," said Faith, "I think I understand."

"He is special."

"It is being a Beta?"

"In part. But there is something about him in particular. He's old, very old. We say *immortal*, but we werewolves rarely see three hundred. Too much fighting – with each other, in armies, with the world. Lyall is, I think, closer to four, and so very calm."

"So, when you fuss and fret, I should take you to him?" Faith sounded like a wife.

Channing laughed. "He also drives me crazy. He is my opposite in so many ways."

"Because you are Gamma?"

"Exactly so. But he has kept me close most of the time since then. And most of the time, I behave because of it. There have been slip-ups, over the years, if he and I are separated for too long. Some Alphas don't understand, and a pack as big as ours is often split for military action. There have been times when I could not protect him as he once protected me. I was not strong enough to be his champion. I hated myself for that and, ironically, couldn't forgive him. We aren't exactly friends and yet…"

Faith's lips twitched. "You're brothers."

"Yes."

"And all that time with no one to love you as you ought to be loved?"

"My appetites do not incline me towards men, and I find it difficult to trust women."

Faith winced, clearly thinking of Odette and the vampire queen. "No doubt. But we're not all so" – her nose wrinkled and she made a face as she searched for the right word – "horrible."

He dipped his head. "No. I begin to think you, at least, are rather unique."

She tilted her head. "What makes you believe, after all that you've done and all that has happened to you, that you are not worthy of me? You move from one to the other. First, no woman is good enough for you, and now you are not good enough for me."

"You are so innocent to be colored by my tawdry history."

"Innocent?" Faith raised both eyebrows.

"You understand my meaning."

"You are forgetting someone in this equation."

"Who?"

"Me. I'm the only one who can truly judge you worthy. You know that, don't you? I'm allowed the freedom and the choice of who to love and who to trust, just as you are. I've chosen you."

She stood and approached him, crouched before him where he sat in the armchair. She put her hands to his knees, his legs only just covered by Biffy's robe.

Her eyes were big and blue and infinite. "We are all messy, fractured beings, muddling through on this great big rock of ours. The choice of what we make of ourselves is what we do with our time here." She shrugged. "I collect rocks. I ache when I hear the cry of a baby. I've looked all my life for family. I thought it was passion. Now I know it is you." She took a breath. "This is what you and I will do now. We will hold these broken parts of ourselves dear because they brought us to this point, and we will love each other wholly and completely. You can rest now. Be with me. Together, we will be enough."

He leaned forward into her. Pressed his wet face into the side of her neck and breathed her in.

She was exactly right; it was enough.

The *Mooning Standard* reported that Miss Faith Wigglesworth married Major Channing Channing of the Chesterfield Channings (yes, he knows) on a misty evening in June in a private ceremony that was, the paper claimed, *very ill attended.*

Invitations were shockingly sparse. Barely three dozen witnessed the ceremony, almost all on the groom's side. This, after such an exciting (and public) courtship, was considered by most to be *very bad form* indeed.

The bride was given away by her cousin, Mr Iftercast. (There was much discussion as to why her parents didn't cross the Atlantic for the event. Claims were made as to the mother's ill health, possible mental instability. Good thing, said the gossipmongers, that this couple could have no children, if there was madness in her blood.) The bride's cousin, Theodora Iftercast, stood up with her, and Professor Randolph Lyall stood with the groom.

The London Pack was present, as were most of its

clavigers. There were no vampires and there were not very many mortals, either. The bride's dress was said to be shockingly simple, and her hat, well, perhaps it was a good thing so few were invited. The hat might have caused a riot. It was a very small white top hat with a veil, but a *gentleman's style* top hat nonetheless.

The Alpha of the London pack was said to be very proud. Particularly about the hat. Whatever that meant.

Faith's husband took great delight in stripping the very silly little top hat, the veil, and the overly simple wedding dress off of her later that night. He did it with such studied care, as if unwrapping a precious gift.

Faith luxuriated in his attentions, certain that shortly, things would flare between them into uncontrollable heat and wonderful violence.

At the beginning, he explored her, gentle and intent on claiming his territory. His hands were cool and occasionally, deliciously, a little rough. His lips were soft and sure, allowing teeth to come out to play when he discovered a sensitive spot. It was glorious.

Then he stood still and let her do the same to him. Not that she hadn't seen it before, but this time there was no sudden nudity, simply pieces of him revealed bit by bit. She took her time to touch, and even kiss and lick a little. When she became brave enough to nibble, he pushed her back, glared, and then showed her how to do it properly.

They ended up standing opposite each other, both entirely naked and free of all encumbrances – made new for each other.

Faith stared at her husband – this fine, handsome man who was hers, who was the pack's, who was a white wolf out of legend.

He tilted his head and she saw the wolf in his eyes.

"Run," he said.

So she did.

She didn't get very far, but she wasn't trying to *actually* escape. She did pretend. She struggled, feeling herself swell and ache and yearn, even as she writhed against him. It was exhilarating and maddening because she wanted so much *more*.

He managed to grab hold of her easily enough, then swept her up and dumped her into the bed – their bed. He loomed over her, captured her wrists in one big hand, and held her down with the comfort of his weight.

And took her.

And kept her.

And gave her everything she yearned for – love and living and fulfillment.

She wrapped herself around him, legs and arms in coils, nails scoring down his back as she struggled still to reach something more, something glorious.

He gave her that, too.

A second heartbeat, she thought, *his heartbeat*, as the pleasure crashed over her.

There was nothing of ice in him then; he melted atop her – liquid, boneless, and prone – entirely hers.

When she grumbled about his weight, he huffed against her neck, where he was nestled, and flipped them both so she was draped over him.

She imagined walking with a white wolf along the tops of the white cliffs of Dover. She imagined the fur against her hand, the ocean scenting the air, and those ice-blue eyes looking up at her.

She looked down into them now, pale-lashed and fathomless, and so very warm.

AUTHOR'S NOTE

Thank you so much for reading *How to Marry a Werewolf*. If you enjoyed it, or if you would like to read more about any of my characters, please say so in a review. I'm grateful for the time you take to do so.

I have a silly gossipy newsletter called the Monthly Chirrup. I promise: no spam, no fowl. (Well, maybe a little fowl and the occasional giveaway.) Join it on my website.

gailcarriger.com

ABOUT THE WRITERBEAST

New York Times bestselling author Gail Carriger writes to cope with being raised in obscurity by an expatriate Brit and an incurable curmudgeon. She escaped small-town life and inadvertently acquired several degrees in higher learning, a fondness for cephalopods, and a chronic tea habit. She then traveled the historic cities of Europe, subsisting entirely on biscuits secreted in her handbag. She resides in the Colonies, surrounded by fantastic shoes, where she insists on tea imported from London.

CPSIA information can be obtained
at www.ICGtesting.com
Printed in the USA
LVOW12s1941210518
577958LV00002B/251/P